MATTHEW MEETS THE MAN

(metaphor)

MATTHEW MEETS THE MAN

WRITTEN and ILLUSTRATED by
TRAVIS NICHOLS

ROARING BROOK PRESS
NEW YORK

Library of Congress Cataloging-in-Publication Data

Nichols, Travis.
    Matthew meets The Man / written and illustrated by Travis Nichols.—1st ed.
        p. cm.
    Summary: As fifteen-year-old Matt copes with freshman year in a Texas high
school, his first girlfriend, and the quest to become a drummer in a band, he
continually confronts authority figures who slow his progress.
    ISBN 978-1-59643-545-2
    [1. Musicians—Fiction.   2. Bands (Music)—Fiction.   3. High school—
Fiction.   4. Schools—Fiction.   5. Dating (Social custom)—Fiction.   6. Family
life—Texas—Fiction.   7. Texas—Fiction.]   I. Title.
PZ7.N544Tam 2011
[Fic]—dc22
                                                                            2010029026

Roaring Brook Press books are available for special promotions and premiums.
For details contact: Director of Special Markets, Holtzbrinck Publishers.

First Edition 2012
Printed in the United States of America by RR Donnelley & Sons Company,
Harrisonburg, Virginia
1 3 5 7 9 8 6 4 2

To my father, Roger, for instilling in me a healthy distrust of entrenched bureaucracies.
To Kip, Tony, and Mike—three irreplaceable pals.

Additional thanks to Deirdre Langeland, Colleen AF Venable, Sarah Eastep, Kayte VanScoy, Jessica Wolkoff, the Faulkenberry Family, Monoe and Pop, Brady and Sam Sloane, and Jennifer Nichols.

Our hero. Yep.

I MEET THE MAN

You know what happens on Thursday afternoons in mid-sized cities in Texas? Nothing. My town, like a lot of places I guess, is like a suburb without a metropolis. A place where the sidewalks roll up at ten p.m. Do you want some good Japanese food at midnight? Well, sure. Dallas is a few hours *that* way, and Austin is a few hours *that* way.

But sometimes boredom and quiet inspire big dreams and creativity. There's a pretty good art scene here and live music almost every week. Touring bands sometimes book shows here to break up the long drive between two larger scenes, and since there isn't much else for people to do, the turnouts are often surprisingly good.

Without a steady stream of metropolitan influence, sure, I'll admit it: I wasn't BORN cool. There was a time when my mom picked out clothes for me, and I was content to mostly sit inside and play video games or trudge around in a creek with my friends. Don't get me wrong, I still love that stuff (except for the mom-picked clothes—that, well, *mostly* ended a long time ago), but something happened to me on what could've been just another Thursday afternoon that made me want more.

MOM-CHOSEN CLOTHES

little logo (armadillo)

braided belt

khaki shorts

tall, white "athletic" socks

off-brand

Windsurfing? Really?

relaxed fit jeans

ironed

Rounding the corner of my block on my way home from school, I wasn't surprised to see Sully in his driveway.

"Hey, Sully."

"Hey, Matt." He looked at the back of my bike. "What's in the case? Cattle prod collection?"

Sully and his family had moved to my town from New York a couple months before, and he always found ways to make little Texas jabs. Of course, he was constantly out in his driveway working on his crapped-out Corvair, which arguably made him much more of a redneck than I'd ever be.

My head scrambled for the perfect "yo momma" joke, but I thought about the fifty pounds and tenure in juvenile hall that Sully had over me and reconsidered. "It's . . . a trumpet," I replied. Yeah, I didn't really know him well enough to "bust his chops," as he puts it.

"Trumpet, huh? That's a shame, kid." I hated when he called me that. Sully was only four years older and two grades ahead of me. "You know, if you played the

10W-30.
Two quarts.

thinking of petty crimes

Five o'clock shadow. Constantly.

pin-up girl tattoo

Sully

drums, you could have your pick of bands to play in. But . . . the trumpet . . . *Neat.*"

Suddenly the trumpet case strapped to my bike weighed a hundred pounds. He was right. I should have fought for my first instinct.

See, in seventh grade, I signed up for band. As in school band, with a band director and chair tests and all of that. When my parents took me to the band hall on orientation day, there was a presentation and some short meetings to sign up for instruments. My dad had raised me on stories of his hot-shot trumpet-playing past, and it was assumed that I would follow in his footsteps.

During the presentation, that went out the window. The demonstrations by the current band were dull at best. I was bored out of my skull through the woodwind and low brass demos. My dad nudged me in the ribs when they brought out the trumpets.

But then another group of older kids came out and lined up behind the percussion equipment in the back of the band hall. They went through a precise, powerful—I don't know— *riff* that filled the room. There were snare drums and cymbals and booming bass drums and those giant timpani things and gongs and all kinds of awesome stuff. That was it: I wanted to be on the drum line. I took about four steps toward the drums before my dad put his arm around my shoulder and steered me to the brass sign-ups. And that was that.

In the car, I had a bit of a tantrum. I'll admit it. I whined about wanting to play drums and how the trumpet was stupid and *wah, wah, wah*. My dad's response rings in my ears to this day, and sounds lamer and lamer each time I remember it. "If your band is playing a gig, and you're the drummer, by the time you're finished packing up all of your stuff, the trumpet player has already left with the good-looking women."

Why did I fall for that load?! I wasn't going to play in some lousy jazz band. My dad just wanted me to carry on the trumpet legacy that he had started when he was a kid. Plus, the fact that he didn't have to spend any money on a new instrument escaped me then, but I'm older now. Don't try to sneak one past me again, Dad.

Now that I'm in high school, being in band means getting to school an hour early every day to march around the practice field in hot, muggy weather, turning blue in the face, and getting red half-circles on my lips. There are all kinds of sharp turns and marks to hit, and I have to make sure that I keep my trumpet bell at the right angle. Oh, *and* I have to play the notes. Meanwhile, the drum line has all the fun in the world. They don't have to march as hard, and they're always laughing and chewing gum and getting, like, respect from the rest of the school. It's cool to play drums. *I* might as well wear a retainer and carry a ferret around with me. What a nightmare.

But that day in Sully's driveway, something occurred to me. Marching band drummers aren't the only people who can play drums in a REAL band—as in a *not-for-school-credit-and-no-uniforms-unless-it's-part-of-your-gimmick* band. In fact, only one of the three drummers I knew of in local bands was actually on the drum line in marching band, and he was a xylophone player. That barely even counts. I could do this—I could be a drummer and have my pick of awesome bands. We could tour and sign to a rad label and make fat stacks of cash. All I needed was a drum kit and a little practice. *Whoa.* I think that's what's called an *epiphany.*

"See you later, Sully!" I started riding fast for home. My house was on the other end of the block, but you know how it is when you have a great idea or really have to go to the bathroom. It felt like it was miles away.

I chucked my bike down on my front porch without un-bungee-ing my trumpet case from the back, plowed through the front door, and rounded the corner into the kitchen. My parents were looking at bills or papers or whatever, and I

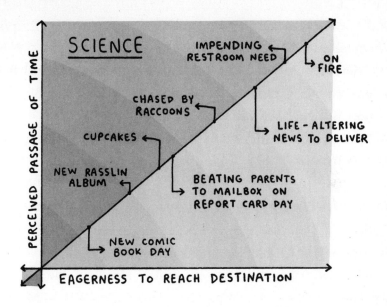

SCIENCE

PERCEIVED PASSAGE OF TIME

EAGERNESS TO REACH DESTINATION

IMPENDING RESTROOM NEED

ON FIRE

CHASED BY RACCOONS

LIFE-ALTERING NEWS TO DELIVER

CUPCAKES

NEW RASSLIN ALBUM

BEATING PARENTS TO MAILBOX ON REPORT CARD DAY

NEW COMIC BOOK DAY

paused . . . then made my proclamation. "Mom. Dad. It is my destiny to be a drummer in a band."

"Matthew, Ma-thew," my dad said. "Remember what I told you. By the time the drummer is finished—"

"I *know*. And I don't mind playing the trumpet. I want to play a drum SET in a REAL band."

"Drums are pretty expensive, dude."

"I know, *dude*. I could get one used online or something. It would just be a few hundred bucks."

My dad's response was the sucking in of air. My mom

didn't even look up from her work. "I don't want you to quit trumpet, Matthew. It's not okay to just quit things."

"I'm not going to quit trumpet, Mom," I said. I could feel my airways constricting. "I want to play drums, too. Not for school. For fun. For *life*."

"I should never have let you quit soccer. That set the precedent for this."

I tapped an invisible microphone. "Is this thing on? Mom. One, I was like five when I quit soccer. Two, I'm not quitting band."

"Okay. I hear that. Just making sure."

My dad recovered from the initial shock of the *idea* of actually having to spend money. "That's a lot of jack, Matt."

"Circles!" I yelled. "We're going in circles here!" I stumbled away from the airless kitchen and made sure to give the front door a really good slam on my way out.

Translation: You were completely terrible and then you became less terrible by a higher margin than others who were terrible and became less terrible.

MOST IMPROVED

Sully was still messing with his car when I trudged back. I told him about the dream-crushing blow I had been dealt. "How the hell am I supposed to get anything I want when my dad is the cheapest guy on the planet, and my mom is always making sure I'm learning something valuable?"

"See this sweet sled?" asked Sully, petting the side of his crusty jalopy like it was a show dog. "I got it for three hundred and fifty bucks from some old weirdbeard on the north side. I had to get it towed to my house. Any day now it'll be up and running, and I'll be picking up preacher's daughters and Miss Texas runner-ups."

"What's your point?"

"My point is, I didn't go crying to my parents for the three-fifty. Or everything I've put in it since to fix it up. I busted hump and got it myself. You know what your problem is?"

receipt for barber school haircut
cologne sample
ARMED
DAD's WALLET

Is it that I'm seeking advice from the oldest junior in the history of Franklin High School?

"Your problem is that you let The Man run your life."

"The man?" I asked. "I just said it's both of them. Dad *and* Mom." What was he babbling about?

"I'm talking about *The Man*. Capital *T*, capital *M*. Authority.

Cops, parents, teachers, bosses, old people. *The Man* is the system of control that keeps its fat thumb pressed down on your freakin' head to make sure you don't have too much fun. In this case, The Man is dear old Mom and Dad trying to keep you from getting a drum kit and having the time of your life."

Sully was making a lot of sense—*again*. I considered alerting the media.

"Look, there's a show in a couple hours at that joke of a pizza place. I'll drive you."

Kaboom. On that Thursday afternoon, I had realized my destiny AND discovered the forces that would try to keep me from it every step of the way. Big day. And it was just getting started.

DESTINY SMELLS LIKE GARLIC AND SWEAT

I told my parents there was a show that night, and that Sully would drive me. There was a slight hesitation, but then I got the go-ahead. They only mildly disapprove of Sully—our dads are friends in that dad way (staring under car hoods together for a few hours on weekends with a six-pack), so I was all set.

It's actually not that hard to get out of the house these days. Since my sister, Beth, is off at college, any time I'm out of the house means no little babies for my folks to take care of. My mom is always rattling on about her soon-to-be-empty nest, but I think my dad is kind of into it: total control of the remote, no crappy music blaring unless it's his crappy music, no greedy mouths eating all the food. I don't blame him. My share of cereal and fruit leather more than doubled in August when Beth moved away.

I crammed my whole ten dollars into my wallet and changed into my favorite T-shirt, a promotional item for an arcade from the late '80s. It's got a space scene and the words "Planet Q Gameporium" in what was once neon green across the front. The shirt was originally black, but was well past charcoal when I got it at the thrift store. After a dozen or so washes, it's pretty much asphalt gray, and it has a few tiny holes in the left sleeve. I'm not allowed to wear it to school (Mom says it's trashy), but it's one of my top choice after-school/weekend shirts. And it only cost me two dollars!

At Sully's house, his dad's massive diesel truck was already chugging along in the driveway. His ol' dad went all out when they moved here. Truck. Cowboy hat. Boots. Thick New York accent. Dallas Cowboys flag in garage. One of these things is not like the others.

"We're taking The Beast tonight, kid," Sully said. "You need a step ladder?"

· · ·

ALL OF THE SHOWS in this bustling metropolis of a hundred thousand or so people take place either at a mini-golf course or in a back room at Gino's by the Slice. There's also a civic center, a big theater, and another big auditorium for concerts, like where my parents dragged me to see Survivor when I was 10 or 11, but I'm talking about shows. For the youngins. By the youngins.

Anyway, Gino's is a pretty cool place. The owner is usually pretty nice about the shows. But he gets irritated when there's a lot of screaming and noise, especially if somebody leaves the door to the back room open. He's afraid of running off the regular, pizza-eating customers. Incidentally, I think the pizza is really good, but apparently it's horrible. Just ask Sully.

"How can people eat this crap?"

"Shucks, mister. I guess us folks down in the sticks don't know no better."

"I bet he's not really from the city. Hell, I wouldn't be surprised if he wasn't even Italian. Worst pie I've ever had."

Sully was the only person from New York that I knew (aside from—allegedly—Gino), and I was confused by some of the things he said. He said "pie" when referring to pizza, "soda" instead of "Coke," and "sneakers" instead of "tennis shoes." Weird. But the strangest and most confusing thing was when he told me he was "standing on line" at the auto shop. *On* line—not *in* it. He was standing *on a line*.

Anyway, the show was amazing. I'd been to shows before, but now I was looking at things differently. People my age and a little bit older were *in bands*. I could *be* one of those guys onstage. Or, in a case like this where there isn't a stage, on *floor*. But you know what I mean.

The first band was a pretty straight-up pop punk group called Susie Muttonchops—Songs about, you know, girls and politics. Mostly girls. They were solid. The vocals were kind of nasal, but the drummer could play super fast. None of the members actually had muttonchops for what I assumed to be pubescent reasons. About half of the younger people at the show were definitely there to see them. You could tell because they headed for the parking lot when the band's set was over. I don't get that. Why pay for a show and only watch one band?

The second band, Sendak Sendak, was from New Mexico. Poppy . . . yet sloppy and rowdy. They didn't have a single piece of equipment that wasn't taped up or dirty or missing a chunk, but they were the five happiest people on the planet. People in the crowd were really getting into the music— some of them were actually dancing, which is really rare for this town. Looking around the room, I was glad to be in that cramped, humid former stockroom with a bunch of grinning kids on the verge of heat stroke. I had to be a part of it.

After Sendak Sendak's set, I went up to the drummer and said, "Nice set." I know—super clever.

"Oh, hey. Thanks, man," he said. He uncapped a jug of water and chugged about half of it.

"So, um, how long have you been playing drums?"

"I started off playing guitar, but our drummer quit, and I switched over. I've been playing for a year and a few months."

"You're kidding."

"Nah, I just filled in for practices while we looked for a replacement, and we just ended up playing a show a couple months after that. I practiced every day. Man, I sucked at first."

What? I was reeling. If I acted quickly, in about a year and a half, not only could I be a great drummer, but I'd also have

a driver's license and could go on tour. Whoa. Whoa. Okay, focus: 1) Drum kit. 2) Band. 3) Car. 4) Adventure.

The last band was another local one. Scabbard . . . something. Can't remember. They played heavy, kind of spacey stuff with a cello player. The music was low, deep, and booming, but the singer sounded like a screeching, dying bird. Awesome, but sort of like listening to math. I think one of the songs was in a 7/12 time signature. I had trouble counting. I laughed to myself when I looked around and watched people trying to bob their heads to the music.

Just as Scabbard _____ was about to play their last song, Gino came busting through the door yelling about—*quelle surprise*—his regular customers leaving because of the screaming. So the show was stopped a few minutes short. I looked around the room. There were about forty attendees there who paid four bucks each to get in. And Gino takes half of the door money at shows. That was EIGHTY bucks. Eighty bucks and he threw a fit. I guess that wasn't enough easy money for our host. Anyway, the awkwardness of the way the show ended gave me the feeling there wouldn't be any more shows at Gino's, now that The Man had shown his face.

Instead of getting some pizza (take THAT, Gino!), I bought a CD from Sendak Sendak's merch table ($5) and got a free button. That plus the four-dollar cover left me with one

dollar. The dollar that would start my drum fund. I smoothed out the wrinkled bill and drew a drum kit under ol' George, which I'm pretty sure is a felony, and vowed to ONLY spend that money on drums. The seed was planted. Now to let that baby grow.

Sully, ever-willing to stick it to 'em, wrote "YER PIZZA SUCKS ANYWAYS!" on a table in the back room. Yikes. I hope he's not my ride on the night he gets taken to jail.

THAT NIGHT I WAS so pumped from the show that I could hardly sleep. I woke up the next morning feeling ragged, but determined to start my plan. I spent about forty-five minutes looking at drums for sale online, and quickly realized that a used kit was the way to go. Still, a lot of the used kits I saw were upward of a thousand bucks. It took some serious searching to find a couple that were doable at only a few hundred. I bookmarked the pages to show my parents later—maybe they'd come around.

THE PUNISH–ED

I had to get ready for school super-quick-style (no shower, clothes from the top of the pile, inhaled cereal, mouthwash instead of brushed teeth), yelled goodbye to my parents over my shoulder, hopped on the Thunder Road (yeah, like you didn't name your bike), and headed to school for morning band practice.

I would have been in my spot on the field on time if the bike rack by the band hall wasn't completely piled with bikes. I had to ride around to the other side of school to lock up. And then, as I was running through the empty hall, I got stopped by the mustachioed assistant principal and got a lecture about running and liability and insurance and a bunch of other nonsense. This guy, this MAN, was making a bad situation worse.

So I nodded and apologized and edged toward the door until I had my hand on the pushbar thingy. Then I just turned and speed-walked down the corridor. As soon as he was out of sight, I started running again.

The band was already doing warm-ups when I hit my spot. I was sweating from the rush and the yeah-it's-barely-eight-a.m.-but-welcome-to-Texas heat, but I had sneaked in late and gotten away with it! Flippin' *score*! Mr. Murphy, the director, was focused on conducting scales. "Daaaaah deee-daaaaaaaah—French horns, watch your tooooone deee-daaaaaaaaah—detention, Mr. Swanbeck—deeeee daaaaaaah . . ."

Crap. The notorious No Tardy Tolerance policy. Without missing a beat or making eye contact. As I struggled to catch my breath, I could've sworn I heard a giggle from a corner of the woodwind section.

I should probably mention Hope Garcia at this point. She's this totally hot clarinet player who I've liked since the first day of summer band practice. She and I hadn't exactly clicked yet. I was working up to it—casual hellos, key adjacent table selection in the cafeteria—waiting for the perfect opportunity to make my move. I certainly wasn't winning any points by getting singled out by one of the school's dweebiest teachers while panting and gasping for air from my cross-campus run.

Sully, the resident hoodlum—a guy who lives on a steady diet of cigarettes, salami, and car fumes—was right. There it was. Twice in the span of five minutes, I had been harassed and embarrassed by The Man for something that was barely my fault. Authority had flexed its pecs and knocked me down a peg. Wow. Was there any hope for The Little Guy?

The rest of band practice was typical. We were working on our halftime show. In just over a week, we'd be marching in the first football game of the season. For me and the other freshmen band-Os, it would be our first high school football game ever. Hoo-ray. I couldn't *wait* to don that thick polyester uniform and plastic shoes. Ah, and what could best top a full suit of itchy, nonbreathable material on a hot Texas night? Let's see . . . oh! How about a plastic hat? Sounds pretty good, but could we stick a big, horrible feather on top of it? SURE! Hey, cool! Thank you!

As we swirled around the field, I kept glancing over at the drum line, and I started to realize something. I was carrying this two-pound trumpet, and they were strapped into half-ton pieces of giant equipment. And you know something, it's not like they were rocking out on *real* drums. Each person had a bass drum or a snare drum or a pair of cymbals or a few toms. I don't know, it kind of seemed like a hassle. They did a lot of sideways marching. As my envy faded, I refocused my thoughts on important things. Getting a drum kit. The formations I was following. Hope Garcia in the corner of my eye (hey, new haircut). Making a farting noise when passing my friends Greg and Andrew on the field. Important things.

The day dragged. Lunch in the cafeteria was a scoop of brown goo, some green goo, and some greasy yellow chunks. Not *completely* disgusting with ketchup on it. Like, all over it.

I grabbed my goo mélange and headed for the usual table, where Greg, Andrew, and Adam were already eating. The three of them have been my best friends since fourth grade. Greg and Andrew play saxophone, and Adam isn't in band. We share a love of video games, strapping Lego men to fireworks, and riding bikes at night. Hey, who doesn't?

As soon as I sat down, I filled them in on my band master plan. I figured they'd want to start a band with me, or at least be into the idea.

"That could be pretty cool," Adam shrugged noncommittally.

"It *would* be," I said. "Tonight we could figure out—"

"I was hoping we could do some questing tonight," interrupted Greg.

"Ooh, yeah," added Andrew. "I really want to try out that new staff."

Flipping *Guilds of Destiny*. They were always playing it. I had played for a while, but it started feeling like what I figured a job felt like. Questing, building up experience, buying equipment, leveling up—it's a lot of work. So I stopped. They still played, though. Constantly. And when they weren't staring at their screens and saving the day, they were messing with their computers' guts. I like games and computers and stuff as much as the next guy, but I couldn't care less about

DNS settings and plugins and ram, or whatever. I just wanted to play the lousy game and get on with my life.

That my friends didn't jump at the idea of starting a band was disappointing to say the least. But I guess I wasn't too surprised. They never came to shows with me. Okay—Adam had come with me *once* when Greg and Andrew were both sick.

I stabbed my lunch with my fork for a few minutes while they prattled on about paladins and spells and other things that I prayed weren't being heard by Hope at the next table.

"Thirty-two inches!" yelled Greg. "Mark it down, sir."

"What?!" Andrew grabbed the ruler out of Greg's hand and hunched over Greg's tray. The uninterrupted line of yellow mustard made a few turns, and Andrew inspected and measured with the intensity of a spinal surgeon. "Fine. Confirmed."

Adam keeps a ledger called *The Book of Records*. The previous record length of mustard from a single packet was twenty-nine and a half inches. A record, until that moment, held by Andrew. Adam flipped to the proper page and made the update.

"All right," I said. "I'll see you guys at Greg's tonight."

When Mr. Murphy gives you detention, you don't go to regular detention. You go to the band hall and stack chairs.

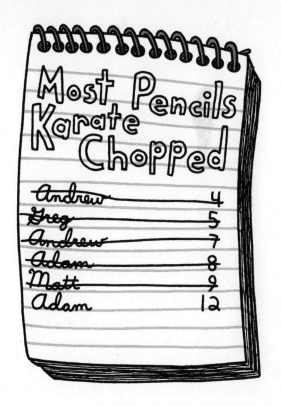

And when you're done with that, you sit and do homework until 4:30. Most of the band kids come through and grab their instruments at the end of the day. When Andrew and Greg came through to get their saxes, Andrew quipped, "The trick to surviving in the joint is to beat somebody up immediately. Establish dominance."

"Out," called Mr. Murphy from his office. "Leave the punish-ed to their punishments; unless you'd care to join them."

They left without another word, and I spotted Hope amid a pack of girls. She looked amazing in a pale green T-shirt and black jeans. Yeah—definitely a new haircut. It was kind of side swept and, I don't know, like the perfect gust of wind just hit it. We locked eyes for a couple of seconds as she passed. Maybe she goes for the bad boys. Note: consider facial tattoo.

Two other kids had band detention that afternoon, so we got everything stacked up pretty fast. It was Friday, which is a long way from Sunday night, so there was no rush on the homework thing. Instead, I drew my ultimate dream drum kit. This thing was a beauty. It was chocolate brown and sky blue with bright white drumheads. Kick, snare, high hat, crash, ride, low tom, middle tom, and high tom. Oh, and a tambourine attached to the high hat stand. I saw that at a show a couple of weeks before. Classy.

One of Mr. Murphy's underling directors saw me drawing and made moves to sound the alarm, but I told him it was a sketch for an art assignment. Sucker.

As I headed out the door after detention, I spotted a drumstick sticking out of a trash can. I nonchalantly put my bag

down next to it and pretended to be looking for something. *Bonus*—the drumstick had a twin. Aside from some dings, I couldn't see anything wrong with them. I did the ol' yawn-and-stretch look-around and quickly put the pair in my bag.

About twenty minutes later, I was home. I started feeling like I was going to get busted somehow for stealing drumsticks, so I took them into the garage and spray-painted them red. I added some black stripes with electrical tape, and holy crap, they looked awesome. They looked custom and rad and in no way like Franklin High School property. Matthew Swanbeck: criminal mastermind.

I still hid them under my mattress. Just in case.

THE DEAD DON'T GET ALLOWANCES

That night, I biked over to Greg's house to find my nerd pals nerding it up in the nerdery. It was kind of stuffy and reeked of nacho cheese. I opened a window. "Remember this stuff?" I asked, taking a deep breath and wafting the breeze indoors. "It's called fresh air. 'Member?"

"How was the slammer?" asked Andrew.

"Honestly, I feel more hardened than rehabilitated," I said. "The system is broken. Also, I found some drumsticks."

"Oh yeah," said Adam. "How was that show last night?"

"Fun. You should have gone." I looked in Greg's direction. "Ciiiiindy was there."

"Hrmph," replied Greg.

"Wait, what's this? Do you like Cindy?" asked Andrew. Uh-oh. I screwed up. Greg's very secretive about girls since Andrew stole his girlfriend in fifth grade.

Greg tried to brush it off. "Nah, I don't know. She's cool, I guess. Adam. Ice barrier. *Ice barrier.*"

So these are my best pals. Stand-up characters. Common interests, but enough differences to keep it interesting. If only they'd unplug from the flipping computers once in a while. Things were better when all we had were bikes and loads of free time. We'd hang out at the creek and make bows and arrows out of branches. That's how I got the two-inch scar on my back that my parents still haven't discovered. Ah, memories.

There wasn't a spare computer, and anyway, I had erased my *Guilds of Destiny* account in a fit of rage a couple of months before, so I just grabbed some snacks and drew for a while. Drums, band logo ideas, diagrams of Adam, Greg, and Andrew.

FINALLY, they were done playing video games for the night, and we snuck out. We walked down to the playground at a nearby elementary school and goofed around for a while.

It got old pretty fast. Andrew let out a power sigh and exclaimed, "Is it too much to ask for a zombie outbreak or *something* to happen around here?"

That prospect livened things up for a minute. We looked around and picked out possible weapons and strategic places to hole up and make a stand. The playground was no good. Too open. We'd get swarmed from all sides. It was decided that if the zombie apocalypse happened right then, we could kick in the door to the gym and grab bats and Frisbees (stay with me). Then we'd bust into the groundskeepers' and custodians' closets for tools and flammable liquids. Finally, we'd get to the cafeteria and secure ourselves behind the locked grates. There we'd have access to (albeit gross) food and water. Spears could be made by duct-taping kitchen knives to broom handles; shovels are pretty good as is. *Destroy the brain.* From there we could even climb the chimney up to the roof and pick off the undead with Molotov cocktails and FIREBALL FRISBEES (there you go). And if we spotted cute (living) girls, we could offer safe haven until the final scene where the military comes with tanks and machine guns.

"If I get infected, promise that you won't hesitate to off me, Matt."

"Same for me, Adam. Same for me."

We waited around for a bit, but there were no signs of a zombie horde. Oh well.

We snuck back into Greg's house and went to sleep.

I WAS THE ONLY one awake at the crack of eleven the next morning, and I walked my bike home instead of riding it. I needed some extra time to think and crunch numbers. Let's see. If I saved every bit of my allowance, an embarrassing, stuck-in-the-'90s eight bucks a week, I could have, like, three hundred dollars in . . . wait, THIRTY-EIGHT WEEKS?! That's no good. This was going to take some creativity.

First off, I had to do something about that measly eight bucks a week. I found my dad in the den watching a riveting show about boats and stepped in front of the TV.

"Matt!"

I took one step to the left. "Dad, we really need to talk about my allowance. It's humiliating. Greg's little brother gets fifteen bucks a week, and he's *nine years old*."

He smiled. "You know what? I think you're right. It's time for a raise."

Was I in the wrong house? Was this really happening? Oh, man. Score!

"I'll have to confer with your mother about this, but I think we can up you to ten dollars a week."

"That's . . . a start, Pappy."

"Dear, can you come in here for a minute?" My mom came around the corner. "Matt and I were just discussing a possible raise in his allowance."

"And . . . what do you think?" she asked.

"I think ten dollars a week is doable. Our son is getting older and more independent."

"I agree. That said, he's old enough to perhaps take on some more responsibilities . . ." Uh-oh.

"Wife of mine, I couldn't agree more." Turning to me, my dad said, "If I can be real with you for a minute, Matty-boy, I grow weary of mowing the lawn. And the best thing about having a strapping young lad such as yourself for a son is that, well, there is no need for me to ever mow a lawn again. For. The rest. Of. My life."

~~10~~ 9 Things I'd Rather Do for an Hour Every Week than Mow the Lawn

- Listen to Beth talk about her latest boyfriend.
- Dust the house. With my face.
- Hang out with Mr. Murphy in a hot car.
- Practice my trumpet in front of a crowd.
- Wash, dry, and fold Sully's laundry.
- Get my cuticles trimmed.
- Hear my mom's "the birds and the bees" talk.
- Listen to classic rock with my dad.
- ~~Eat beans. No, listen. I HATE BEANS.~~
- Swing dance at the senior citizens' center.

"But, Dad. I *do* mow the lawn sometimes."

"And starting tomorrow, you'll mow it every week to earn that sweet, sweet raise. And when winter comes, we'll find some other things you can do instead."

Mom stepped in to seal the deal with a good lesson. "This will be good for you, Matthew; hard work, responsibility."

I turned to leave. Mowing the lawn every week for an additional . . . eight bucks a month. Hardly seemed worth it. And then my dad put the final nail in the coffin.

"One more thing, fruit-o-m'loins. This raise means no extra money here and there for movies or games or snacks. If you want it, save up for it. You'll thank me later."

"I'll thank you now, *Man*."

"You're welcome, man."

"That was a capital *M*, Dad!"

Clearly, raising cash was going to take some extra effort. The record store near the mall buys used CDs, and I had a bunch of junk from before I got into, well, good music. I don't even want to list the stuff in my collection. It's . . . bad, okay? I gathered up about twenty-five real stinkers and switched the cracked cases with nicer ones from CDs I was keeping. Used CDs at the record store sell for eight to ten bucks a piece, so I figured they'd buy mine for close to a hundred bucks total, and that would really beef up the drum fund. Cha-ching!

But The Man at the record store had different ideas.

"I'll give you fifteen."

"Are you *serious*?" My CDs had been divided into three little stacks on the counter.

The manager didn't even blink. "Yep. These are a buck fifty, and these are a dollar, and I can't take these."

"But you sell them for, like, ten bucks."

"It's called profit margins, kid. I have overhead. Now take it or leave it, but if you're going to tell me how to run my—"

"I'm sorry, sir." *Sir?* "I didn't mean to . . . I'll take the fifteen dollars. Thank you."

I took my money and the stack of CDs he didn't want and left. What a scam.

AS I BIKED HOME, it occurred to me that I hadn't eaten all day. I stopped for a burrito and a snow cone. Yeah, I spent money that should've gone to the drum fund, but hey, it could be the last snow cone of the season. They're not open year-round, and the snow cone lady is like a surrogate mother to me.

When I got home, I pulled my drumsticks from under my mattress and tried to play a simple beat on my bed. It wasn't great. Crap. That couldn't be the end of it. I had to make it super official. I took an empty one-gallon pickle jar from the kitchen and taped my seed dollar from the night before on the side. On a strip of masking tape, I wrote "DRUM FUND" and stuck it above my first dollar. I put in the ten bucks and change from my CD sales minus the burrito and the snow cone, and scrounged around my room (and in the couch cushions in the den) and found another $1.56 in loose change.

You know what? Not a bad start.

WORKING FOR THE MAN

A few days later, my mom called me into the kitchen.
"Matthew, I just talked to your Uncle Kyle. I told him that
you're trying to save up some money, and he wants to offer
you an after school job at his restaurant. Call him back."

"Oh . . . cool." I'd segue with *little did I know . . .* , but I
did know. I completely knew. But I made the call, anyway.

The next day, I had my apron, two official T-shirts and
a small, white towel. My uncle's restaurant is a Mexican

seafood place called Pepe's. Yeah. Aside from the name being totally weak, it's . . . Mexican seafood. Like 400 miles from Mexico or the ocean. Between you and me, I question both the authenticity and freshness, so I only eat chips, salsa, and guacamole when my family drags me there dang near every Sunday. For that reason, Uncle Kyle always scowls at me. I once overheard him say to my dad, "That kid is just, just *weird*." Aaaaaand then he became my employer.

Ol' Kyle parades around the joint like a big shot, bossing everybody around. That first day, I learned loads of great Spanish swears while hanging around in the kitchen. I'd be back there scraping dishes, and Kyle would burst in and yell, "*Vamanos, amigos! Andale!*" at the staff, clapping his hands in the air. They wouldn't even look up at him. Then he'd leave, and whoa, those guys would let it fly. I really look up to them. The Man might sign their checks, but they don't suck up to him. Meanwhile, *I* still have to write him thank-you notes after Christmas and my birthday, even when he gives me button-up shirts or cologne.

I tried to hide that he was my uncle by calling him "Mr. Lindstrom," but it only took about twenty minutes for him to call me *sobrino* (Spanish for "nephew") when I was refilling some chip bowls. It's bad enough that he embarrassed me and ruined any chance of my keeping a low profile, but why does

he insist on tossing Spanish words around like that? He's a flipping Swede, for crying out loud.

Filling and refilling bowls of chips and salsa was the least offensive part of the job. I also had to clear off finished plates and scrape them in the kitchen before putting them in the dishwasher. And I had to wipe down tables with my towel and, this is the worst part, carry the towel around for the entire shift. I could rinse it off and wring it out in the back, but I still had to have this warm, moist rag over my shoulder. Sick. I didn't know how I was going to handle working there. Two or three dinner shifts a week on school days and longer shifts on Saturday and/or Sunday depending on football games. I figured I could quit as soon as I got my first paycheck. Then I'd buy my drums and start making money playing shows. Freedom in two weeks, I told myself. *Two weeks.*

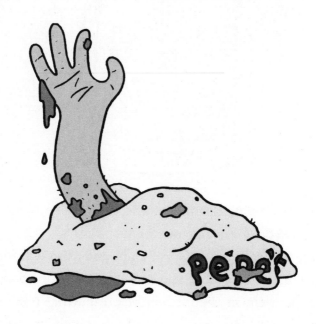

GOOD CITIZENS OF THE REPUBLIC

After weeks of early mornings of countless run-throughs and practices, it was finally the night of the first football game of the season. I'm not a big sports fan, but I figured I'd have fun up in the stands anyway. And, you know, I was actually kind of excited to march in a halftime show—although I still wasn't stoked about the uniform.

It turned out to be a lot of work up in the stands. All of those short non-halftime songs we'd been practicing? We played them; something every few minutes. And even though the sun was completely down halfway through the first quarter, we were all sweating like crazy.

In September, national clothing chains wheel out the light scarves and "summer sweaters." I don't know who's in charge of regional research for these companies, but where I live, September is *not* sweater weather. My poly/steel/wool blend uniform clung to me like a plastic tarp. I suddenly got an idea: short-sleeved uniforms. I whipped out my little sketchbook

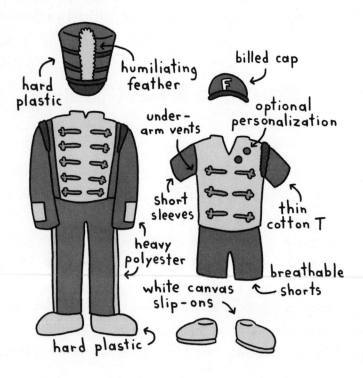

hard plastic

humiliating feather

billed cap

optional personalization

under-arm vents

short sleeves

thin cotton T

heavy polyester

breathable shorts

white canvas slip-ons

hard plastic

and pen and drew it out. As we walked down the stands to the field for halftime, I showed it to Mr. Murphy.

"See, they look pretty much the same, but the short-sleeved cotton shirts and shorts are more breathable. They'd probably help us march more smoothly. Especially with white slip-on canvas shoes and—"

"Mr. Swanbeck, please get in line. And don't bring that to any more games. Focus." I'd been shot down by a Man in a short-sleeved polo shirt and khakis. He had no idea what we were going through.

The halftime show went okay. It was pretty sloppy in parts, but it was our first performance. At one point, about ten of us (second and third trumpets, most of us freshmen) missed our marks by an itty-bitty five yards and had to hustle over to where we were supposed to be. But all in all, I thought it went really well.

Mr. Murphy disagreed. We all got a lecture about paying attention and watching our marks and keeping our bells up and (looking and pointing directly at me) "doodling and farting around in the stands." The student section to our left and the parents section to the right got to hear it all, too. I felt about three hundred pairs of eyes on me. Being hassled by The Man is even more thrilling when it's in public.

• • •

AFTER THE GAME, my pals and I decided that we should stay out all night and TP some houses. Specifically, Hope's and Cindy's. In some cultures, when a boy likes a girl, he buys her flowers. What a world. Anyway, Andrew and Adam told their parents they were staying at Greg's house, and Greg and I told our parents that we were staying at Andrew's house. I grabbed all of the bills and quarters from my drum fund jar and met back up with my friends down the street from Andrew's house. I know what you're thinking—looting my own drum fund. But I had to get supplies. And the big payoff from Pepe's was coming up, so I wasn't worried.

The first thing we did was gear up at the drug store. My mom is a total tree hugger, and she's managed to pound some of her ethics into my brain.

"We should get this kind," I said.

"Dude, that's like three bucks more a pack!" Adam—ever the miser.

"I know, but it's recycled and unblea—"

Andrew rolled his eyes. "Here we go again. Fine, but you're paying extra."

"Whatever."

I also spotted a battery-powered toy drum set in the toy aisle. It had four pads that you actually hit with sticks. The

46

sound was terrible, but I figured it would be good practice, and it was only twenty bucks. Goodbye, saved allowance and scrounged change. The drum fund would basically be back to zero, but in a week and a half, I'd be getting a paycheck from the restaurant. No worries.

We loaded the toilet paper into our backpacks—I had *six rolls* crammed in my bag. That's some major mayhem.

Cindy's house was up first. "Don't worry," Andrew told me as we pulled out the ammunition. "We'll wreck your dream girl's house, too."

Greg put his hand on my shoulder. "Sorry, man. He's onto you. Better act fast before he steals her."

We did a pretty amateur job in Cindy's front yard, but she didn't really have a lot to work with. Just one medium-sized pecan tree and some bushes. Honestly, I wasn't proud of the work. I'd give it "two rolls." I wouldn't put it on my résumé.

Cindy's house

I got really nervous on the way to Hope's house. When walking around at night, my usual modus operandi is to act casual if a car passes. Adam also keeps pretty calm. The idea is that if you act like you're not doing anything wrong, passers-by won't assume you're up to anything. But that night I dove for cover twice right alongside Greg and Andrew.

It was after midnight when we made it to Hope's house and started unloading the rest of our toilet paper. She's got four big trees in her yard, so it was looking really good.

Hope's house

I was just a few feet away from a big front window, masterfully wrapping a rosebush, when I heard movement inside the house. I turned and saw the outlines of two people behind a pulled back set of mini-blinds.

"GUYS!" I whisper-yelled.

Greg and Andrew instantly dove behind the air conditioner on the side of the house, and Adam stood frozen behind a tree. I held my breath for what seemed like an eternity. Then, the garage door began to open, and a car backed out into the driveway and onto the street. As it rounded the corner, a girl's voice called out from the back seat, "You're toast, Matthew! TOOOOOOAST!"

After our hearts started beating again, we packed up the leftover rolls and skulked back to the drug store so we could buy some drinks. A police car pulled up to us in the parking lot just before we went inside. "You boys are out pretty late."

"Yes, sir . . ." Greg croaked.

"Now I know we don't have a youth curfew, but the way I see it, kids your age don't have any business walking the streets at this hour."

"We're just getting something to drink," said Adam.

"I don't recall asking, son," snorted the cop. "Now I've got half a mind to call all your parents, 'cause I'd bet they don't know ya'll are out here."

"Officer," I said. "We're sorry. We were excited about the football game tonight. We'll go straight home."

He paused. "All right. I better not see you again."

He put his cruiser into drive and sped off. We were still fuming after we got our drinks and began walking back.

"I guess all of the murders and robberies have been solved, and they have time for this piddly stuff," barked Adam.

I chugged my apple juice and put the bottle in my bag. "Yeah, what the crap? We're the good kids. We get good grades. We're not doing anything wrong, but The Man can't *not* hassle."

"Well," replied Andrew. "We *did* just trespass, litter, and vandalize."

Adam let out a huge belch. Reaching into his backpack, he

said, "And then there's this . . ." He flicked a lighter, and the fuses of an entire 100-pack of Black Cats sparked and hissed. He chucked them into the street and flashed a toothy smile. We bolted down the alley, barely able to stifle our laughter and swears, and soon it was like a machine gun going off around the corner.

It was just past one a.m., and we didn't have anything else planned for the night. Unfortunately, we didn't really have anywhere to go, either. We were each supposed to be at someone else's house. We decided to settle in at the playground. I managed to wedge myself inside a curvy slide and doze off for a couple hours.

As soon as the sun started coming up, we headed over to Andrew's house to raid the pantry. His dad was already awake and making pancakes. "Sorry, chumps. I only made enough for me. Why are you home so early?"

"Greg's family is going out of town or something . . ." Andrew hardly tried to hide things from his dad.

"Yeah," said Greg. "I better get going."

"Uh-huh," said Andrew's dad. He didn't care at *all*. It occurred to me that it wouldn't have been a big deal to go to Andrew's house in the middle of the night to sleep instead of giving myself scoliosis at the playground.

I wanted to get going, too. Crashing on my bed for about eight hours sounded like the best thing in the world.

About two blocks from my house, though, I thought I could faintly smell cinnamon. As I got closer, the smell got stronger. And then I saw it: The trees in my yard—completely wrapped in baby blue toilet paper. Cinnamon-scented.

"Oh, good," said my mother from the driveway. "You're home early. You can clean this up before you go to work."

My house

PROVERBIAL PIGTAILS PROVERBIALLY DIPPED IN THE PROVERBIAL INKWELL

If you're taking notes (and I trust that you are) write this down: If you're 14 and you want to attract a particular young lady or young man, well, mess up their house.

My crappy weekend of wiping tables, scraping plates, loading the power washer, unloading the power washer, stacking the boiling hot dishes, and filling salsa bowls at Pepe's was an almost unbearable assault on my senses. But on Monday afternoon, I got some awesome and unexpected news.

"Hope likes you, you know." I turned from my locker to

see Cindy standing next to me. She was smacking her gum as if it were fighting back.

I had to remember how to make my brain form words. "That's . . . I . . . oh."

"So do you like her?"

Be cool, Matt. "Yas." It was a cross between yes and yeah. Loser.

"Good. So ask her to homecoming. And to the movies or whatever." She was really attacking that gum.

My stomach found its way back in place. "I mean, Hope and I have said like ten words to each other ever, so I don't really know what to do. But, um, okay. Thanks."

"Sure. By the way, you guys suck. My mom made me clean up our yard by myself. It was gross."

"Yeah, sorry about that."

"No, you're not."

"You're right."

"Whatever. We got you back. Hope's cousin is like a monkey. She was up in your trees and everything. All right. Ask Hope out."

She turned to walk away, and then, as selfless and giving as I am, I suddenly thought of someone other than myself.

"What about you?" I asked.

"What about me what?" she smacked.

"Are you, like, going to homecoming with somebody?"

"I don't know yet. Maybe with David. He hasn't asked, but I heard he might."

Uh-oh. She was talking about David Egerton, a junior. Tromboner. It was only a month into the school year, and the upper-classmen were already starting to pounce on the fresh-men. I made a note to talk to Greg and let him know that he needed to hurry the hell up if he wanted a chance.

But back to me. I stood at my locker trying to figure out my next move with Hope, and didn't even notice the tardy bell for second period.

"Let's *move* it." It was that dang assistant principal with the 'stache. "Your education is at stake!"

"Yes, Mr. . . . um, yes, sir." But there was more at stake than my education. Hope was in my next class.

AFTER FIFTY MINUTES of staring at this little tiny mole on the back of Hope's right arm and watching her twirl her pen over her fingers (everyone on the debate team does that, and I have no idea how—it's pretty spectacular), the bell rang, and the classroom started emptying out.

"Hey, Hope?" I swear, I was totally on autopilot. I don't even remember psyching myself up to say that. I suddenly realized what I was doing and prayed to the gods of teenhood for a squeak-free voice and that my hands weren't shaking noticeably.

"Hi, Matthew."

"Listen, I was wondering if you wanted to go to a movie or something this weekend. It's cool if you don't."

"Sure. That sounds fun."

And then, I don't even know how I got so freaking smooth all of a sudden. "Also, I wanted to thank you for helping make our compost bin smell so good."

"You're welcome. Two things. One, that's not our, um, normal . . . I mean, my cousin bought that stuff last week for a prank, and she had a ton left over. Two, if Cindy told you . . . anything, I didn't tell her to."

I stuck with the first thing on her list. "Okay, good. Because in that context, blue cinnamon toilet paper is hilarious. But otherwise, it's—"

"Completely weird. I know."

"I DON'T GET IT. How did you ask?"

"I just . . . asked."

"Oh. Wow."

After school, my friends were hanging out at Pepe's doing the chip scheme while I worked. The way the chip scheme works is that you go to a restaurant that serves complimentary chips and get a table for one more person than you have with you. So, in Andrew, Greg, and Adam's case, they asked for a table for four. Then you sit and eat chips and salsa and look at the menu and periodically say out loud, "Golly, where *is* he/she?" and "Gosh, I don't know. It just goes straight to voice mail!" And you tell the server that you want to wait until your fourth arrives to order. Then, finally, you give up and tell the server you're going to just leave.

And, to not be total jerks, you leave a few bucks on the table. When I think about it, it's a pretty weak scheme. I mean, why would you leave just because one person didn't show up? It's stupid, but it works.

The server (Joanna) who seated my friends had figured out pretty quickly that they weren't going to order any food, but she didn't really mind. They had ordered cokes, so *technically* they were paying customers, and when she went to get their drinks, I followed her into the kitchen and assured her that they'd tip her. She didn't care. It was one less table for her to mess with on a slow shift.

After refilling some chip bowls, I wandered back to my friends' table.

"YAAAAA! How fast was that?" Andrew was slouched over his empty glass and clutching his forehead.

"Four and a half seconds. It's a new record." Adam crossed through a line on an open page in *The Book of Records*. The previous large-coke drinking record was five and a half seconds. Held by me. I rushed to the drink machines so I could attempt to reclaim my title.

My uncle stopped me and called me into his office. "Matthew. I gave you a job as a family favor. But that doesn't mean you get special treatment. If anything, I expect more from you."

"Kyle, I—"

"Your friends can't distract you from your work. Thin ice, *sobrino*. You're on thin ice."

I was fuming, but I swallowed the rage. In no time at all, I would get a WELL-DESERVED paycheck, and I could quit.

"*Lo siento, tio. Que no vuela a ocurrir.*" (Thanks, kitchen staff.)

"What?"

"Mom wants to know if you want to have lunch with her this week."

"All right, I'll give her a call. As for you, there are dishes stacking up in the kitchen."

When I left Kyle's office, my friends were gone. Joanna came over and handed me four crumpled one-dollar bills.

"They left me ten bucks tip on a five dollar tab. I know Kyle's your uncle and all, but he's kind of a jerk."

"I know. Sorry."

"Whatever, man. It's dead out there. I don't care."

AFTER WORK, I figured it was time to remind myself why I was putting myself through that assault to my senses. Back in my room, I pulled out my toy drum set. It pretty much sounded like crap, but I felt like it was actually helping me begin to get

some skills. I found some online videos of beginner drum lessons, which helped me figure out the correct way to hold my sticks, what I should hit with which hand, and stuff like that. I was watching and listening to the videos with headphones on, and I got the idea to practice along with music by using two sets of headphones. I plugged some earbuds into either my computer or my MP3 player, and then plugged bigger headphones into the headphone jack on the drum kit. That way I could layer headphones in and on my ears and hear the music and what I was playing at the same time. The only downside was double EMFs in my brain. I promised myself I'd stop if I got a nosebleed or started tasting copper.

The toy drums only had kick, snare, crash, and handclap pads, and none of them sounded like what they were supposed to be. But it was four different sounds. I figured that by the time I had my real drum kit, I'd be pretty good.

THE COURTSHIP OF MS. GARCIA AMID
FEAR OF MURDER

By the time Friday rolled around, my date with Hope had become a double date with Greg and Cindy. He had manned up and asked her out. I couldn't believe it. To be fair, the situation was kind of forced. Hope's parents weren't stoked at the idea of their daughter dating, especially since they had never met me. So I volunteered Greg, and she volunteered Cindy. It was a "group thing." Done deal. Oh, and I had to meet her parents.

"So you must be Matthew." Hope's mother stood in the

doorway in baby blue medical scrubs with a pattern of kittens and balls of yarn. "Come in, come in."

Hope was sitting next to her dad on a huge leather couch. "Mr. Swanbeck. Welcome to our home. Sit. Talk."

I chose a seat in a facing armchair. "Thank you, Mr. Garcia. And Mrs. Garcia."

"Dr. Garcia. She's a doctor."

"Oh, right. Sorry. Dr. Garcia."

"John, leave the young man alone," said Dr. Garcia. "Should he call you 'Mr. Garcia, Esquire' as well?"

"Has a nice ring to it. I paid a lot for that title. So tell us about yourself, Matthew."

I went through a little prepared spiel about good grades and going to church and playing trumpet in band and art classes and volunteering at a nursing home (which is kind of true—I went to youth group at church a couple of times when I thought there was going to be a pizza party or bowling, but it turned out to be hanging out with the residents of Sunset Meadows).

"Fine, fine, fine," said Hope's dad. "What are you kids up to this evening?"

Hope fielded that question. "We're meeting the rest of the group at the theater, seeing a movie, and then getting something to eat."

"Sounds good. Maria, are you dropping the kids off at the theater?"

"Yeah," Hope's mom said, getting up. "I'll pull the car around."

Hope and I stood up, but her dad said, "You go ahead, Hope, dear. I want to show Matthew my trophies."

Hope rolled her eyes. "Dad."

"It's fine, it's fine. I'll send him right out." Hope headed out the front door, leaving me with the scariest Man I've ever met. Then he turned to me. "She can make it look like an accident, you know."

Oh, crap. "What's that, sir?"

"My wife. She can make what happens to you look like an accident, and then I'll see that the paperwork gets quickly and quietly processed. It's that easy."

"Sir, I . . ."

"BWAHAHA! Relax. You're a good kid. Seriously, though. Respect her. And know that I have eyes all over this city."

We stood, and he shook my hand. He didn't over-squeeze in a too-macho way, but I could tell that he could have completely destroyed my hand at any moment.

"Nice meeting you," he said. "I'll be seeing you. Oh, yeah. My trophies. On the shelf to the left of the front door."

"It was nice meeting you, too, sir." I turned toward the exit

and took my first breath in ten minutes. Just past a dozen pictures of a tiny Hope in ballerina outfits with her hair pulled up in a little bun and others where she stood with gymnastics ribbons, I saw the trophy shelf. The awards were all for martial arts tournaments that Mr. Garcia, *Esquire*, had won. Oh, and there was a photo of him smashing like ten concrete blocks with the hand that just shook mine.

THE CAR RIDE WAS a lot less overtly scary, but all the way to the theater I kept running through the possible scenarios of Dr. Garcia "making it look like an accident."

"What field of medicine do you practice, Dr. Garcia?" I finally asked.

"I'm a radiologist."

Okay, X-rays and stuff. Not quite as easy access to traceless poisons. Anyway, I guess I wasn't *actually* fearing for my life. I remember how my dad used to act when boys came over to take Beth out. Once he even left a shotgun out. He looked at it, stared hard at the guy and said, "Pardon the mess." Yeah, completely cliché. Cliché but effective. That kid was terrified.

Dr. Garcia pulled up to the front of the theater and looked back at me through the rearview mirror. "All right. I'll pick you kids up here at 10:15."

"Thanks, Mom."

"Thanks, Dr. Garcia."

At the movie, Hope and Cindy sat next to each other, and Greg and I sat on either side. I had saved a ton of cash by meeting up with Greg right after school to buy snacks and drinks at a grocery store. And instead of it looking like we were cheap, we were fun and dangerous. A couple of rebels sneaking in food. And the kind of stuff you can't get in a theater: ginger ale in glass bottles, fancy granola bars, and lots of minty gum. Because you never know.

It got awkward when Greg and Cindy started making out halfway through the movie—and not stopping at all until the credits rolled. Hope and I hadn't even held hands or anything. And it was impossible to make a move with SlobberFest going on in the corner of my eye.

The lights came up and a gangly usher came through to clean. We were packing up Greg's backpack when the usher saw our bottles. "Outside food and drink is not allowed in the theater. *Especially* alcohol. I should call the police. You'll all get MIPs!"

Wow. It seemed that this guy had a power complex. "It's *ginger ale*," said Hope.

"F-fine, but *like I said*, outside food and drink are NOT ALLOWED inside the theater."

"We're sorry. We're leaving anyway, and—"

"You're leaving and not coming back. What are your names?"

"That's not necessary," I offered. "We won't do it again."

"You certainly won't. Not in *my* theater." I wasn't convinced that he had any real authority, but just as I was about to say so, Hope snapped back.

"Maybe if a small watered-down coke wasn't five bucks *after* paying ten bucks each for tickets, people wouldn't bring things in." Wow. Hope—sticking it to that tool of The Man. And she was with *me*.

He pulled out his walkie-talkie to, I suppose, call a manager. "Little girl, you are all banned from this theater and all theaters in our chain."

That did it. "Whoa, whoa, whoa," I said. "Come on. 'Little girl?' That's out of line. And banning us from the entire corporate chain? We all know that's not something you do." He stared blankly at me. I stood up and motioned for the group to leave. "Now," I said, "do you guys have recycling bins, or do we need to take these with us?"

EVEN THOUGH I could've gotten us a discount at *Pepe's*, which was only a couple of blocks away, I didn't want to see my uncle or anyone I worked with. So we walked a little bit farther to a Thai place. I had never had Thai food before. Hope promised me it was "like Chinese food but with less fried stuff and with better sauces." She almost lost me at "less fried," but I like sauce. I got some noodle-y stuff with peanuts and sprouts and junk. It was really good.

cilantro-
tastes soapy

lime

noodles

flower-
to eat?

sprouts

assorted
chunks

peanut crumbs

The four of us talked about band and school. Greg kept video game talk to a minimum, which was smart. I told Hope that I was saving up for a drum set, and she thought that was cool.

When we were all finished, the server came by and started collecting our plates. He said, "Any dessert? Mango sticky rice for you or your girlfriends?"

Hope didn't correct the server by saying she wasn't my girlfriend. I took that as a good sign.

When the check came, Greg and I snatched it off the table before the girls could make any attempt to try to pay at all. Hope had tried to go for it. Cindy—not so much.

Hope said, "Thanks, Matt. I'll buy next time." She said *next time*. So I knew I was set.

As we were walking back to the theater for our rides, the group split up. Hope and I walked ahead of Greg and Cindy, who were no doubt making out again in some bushes or something. I used that, our only moment alone, to ask Hope to homecoming.

"I don't know if you already have plans or anything, and it's cool if you do, but if you don't, and you want to, um, would you go to homecoming with me?"

"Well, of *course*," she said, giving me a huge hug.

The timing was perfect, because just then, the car pulled up.

"Oh, hello, young people," said Mr. Garcia.

The car ride home was completely uncomfortable.

"It's okay," said Hope. "I convinced him that we weren't making out or anything." It was Saturday afternoon, and we were in our band uniforms and loading up buses to march in our first away game.

"Okay, good. I really want your dad to like me. I mean, it would be easier that way."

"He likes you. I told him that you opened doors for me and paid for dinner. That's a big deal to him. And yeah, I told him that I was just hugging you. We weren't making out."

"Good, because I'd hate for—"

"Yeah, I said you didn't even try to kiss me or anything. Didn't put the moves on me at all. Not. At. All. Total gentleman."

"Well, now you're just embarrassing me," I said.

"Settle down."

So, on the bus I made sure we were out of sight and sound range of Greg and Cindy, and I held Hope's hand like a champ for most of the three-hour bus ride.

The game itself was just like a home game. The differences were the coming and going. Instead of sweating in our uniforms on the un-air-conditioned bus for twenty minutes after the game (the trip from the stadium back to school), we got to sweat in them for a few hours. We got to take the top halves off and ride back in our too-cool high-high-high-waisted pants and suspenders over our T-shirts. I was rocking my amazing (-ly terrible) "My Grandparents Went to Hawaii and All I Got Was This Lousy T-shirt" shirt. Hope had on a nice white V-neck shirt, and I prayed that she didn't suddenly realize that she was ten times cooler than me.

THE RIDE HOME was like a teen exploitation movie. The band directors and sponsors sat at the front of each bus and left a bunch of sweaty kids to their devices in the dark. I mean, not exactly. Every once in a while, an adult would walk down the aisle. The guy doing the rounds on our bus was a parent. He even said, "Hand check! Heh, heh, heh . . ." Creep.

I don't really like talking about this kind of stuff, and I don't really want to get into it, but Hope and I made out a little bit. Nothing serious. It's just, yeah. Shut up. The point is, after a few minutes, I heard a screeching voice a few feet from my face.

"THEY'RE KISSIN'!"

I looked up and saw the snotty face of some little pixie-haircutted elementary school kid.

Hope didn't miss a beat. "Well, aren't you a little tattle-tale?"

"Nuh-uh! I'm not tattlin'! I'm helpin' Daddy."

"Tsk, tsk, tsk," I said. "So young, and already a tool of The Man." With that, the kid left to pursue more interesting endeavors—booger eating, pants wetting, etc.

I looked back at Hope. Even with her hair sticking to her neck—even in those dreadful blue pants up to her armpits, she was really beautiful. Maybe even more beautiful because of those things. Oh, jeez. Does that make me some sort of pervert?

"So anyway, Matthew," said Hope. "Two things. One, I

guess you're pretty much my boyfriend now. Two, my parents now have reason to murder you."

HAVING A GIRLFRIEND makes school a completely different experience. There's note-writing, lunches together, hand-holding in the halls. Hope could be talking to someone, and I could be having a completely separate conversation with someone else, and we'd be holding hands but otherwise not even acknowledging each other. Totally weird. I saw monkeys on TV acting in a similar way. Two monkeys in a tree—one was eating bugs and sort of just hanging on the other who is absentmindedly pulling leaves off a branch.

At any rate, it's rad.

THE MAN IS A THIEF!

A few days later, the moment I had been waiting for finally arrived: my paycheck at work. I had worked about twenty-two hours in the pay period, so I'd be getting around $160. That was PLENTY of money to really make the drum kit happen. After a few weeks of mowing the lawn and being thrifty, I could get a passable used kit, and I could quit my stupid job.

I pictured the adoring crowds. Rumbling toms and crashing cymbals. Touring. Freedom. Hope working the merch table.

Or maybe playing clarinet in the band with me—*nah, that's no good*. I tore open the envelope to reveal my golden ticket.

"What the—96.47?!"

"Problem, *sobrino*?"

"*Yeah*, there's a problem! My paycheck is all jacked up. Some *FICA* thing stole like thirty bucks from me, and then something called 'restaurant apparel' took *another* thirty!"

My uncle chuckled at his desk. "FICA is a tax for Social Security and Medicare. It's automatically deducted. It's for when you retire or—"

"But I didn't approve that! Can't I just get the money? I'm trying to save up for drums, and if I have to wait until I retire to get the money I'm owed, I'll be too old to play. This is so stupid."

"Oh, you poor, poor boy. I'm afraid it doesn't work that way."

"Well . . . well . . . what's this 'restaurant apparel' thing?"

"When you started working here, you were given two *Pepe's* T-shirts and an apron. And the cost is taken from your first check. I told you that. You don't pay attention, Matthew."

"This just isn't what I expected at all," I said.

"Welcome to the real world, *sobrino*. Don't worry. Over

winter break, and again in the summer, you can work up to 35 hours a week."

Oh . . . oh, no.

"YOUR FIRST PAYCHECK! Oh, this is exciting. I mean, for you, sure. But for *me*. I mean this is *thrilling*!" My dad was holding my check like it was the Holy Grail or something. "This is one step closer to your financial independence. Maybe you can buy your own school supplies and clothes now. Ooh! The savings! I can buy a boat!"

"Dear, that's enough," said my mom. "Matthew, this is a big moment for you. You're learning a lot about the principles of work and earning and—"

"Why can't he just pay me in cash under the table?" I whined. "I'm his *nephew*, for crying out loud."

My dad laughed. "With the INS and the IRS breathing down his neck? Fat chance, buddy boy."

"And this brings to mind something your father and I have been talking about. We know that you're saving up for drums, and that's great. We want to help you."

"OH MY GOD! THANK YOU SO—"

"Now, hold on, Matthew," interrupted my dad. "We want to help you, but even more so, we want to help you *appreciate* your drums when and if you get them. So we're taking a position of stepping back. If you truly want drums, you're going to have to save up for them yourself."

"Oh."

"You see, Matthew," continued my mom, "working for them will make you really value them."

"Right," agreed my dad. "Plus, we've footed the bill for a dozen of your flights of fancy. Magic classes, fencing lessons, pottery classes, kung fu, unicycle, fighter kite. Shall I continue?"

"No, thanks."

THE EVOLUTION OF ANCIENT RITUALS
AND APPLICATION TO MODERN SOCIALIZING

This was the first time I had a date at homecoming (a lot of middle schoolers went to high school football games, but I was never into it), so I was really nervous. And then nervousness became anxiety. Money anxiety. I realized I had to get Hope a mum.

If you're not familiar, a homecoming mum is a giant fake flower draped with tacky ribbons and dumb little ornaments, all in school colors. Sometimes they even have *two* fake flowers in the middle. Guys are supposed to make them or buy them and give them to their dates. And the girls pin them on and wear them to school on the day of homecoming, at the football game, and then at the homecoming dance after that. It's a horrible, horrible tradition. Sully's mind was completely blown by the notion (apparently they don't have homecoming mums in New York), and assured me that juniors and seniors didn't participate, but that's no help to a freshman. It was expected. And potentially expensive, especially if you buy them already made. I had to make this thing.

I biked to the hobby store and bought a flower-thing, a handful of ribbons, two little football charms, a bell, and a set of stick-on letters to spell "Hope" and "Matthew." (Thankfully the set came with two *E*s and two *T*s.) I played it super cheap, but was still out $17. Why couldn't I have started dating Hope *after* getting my drums? Or at least after homecoming.

I SPREAD MY stuff out on the kitchen table and assembled the mum. It was skimpy—okay, it was really skimpy, but it had to do. I mean, Hope and I hadn't been seeing each other for that long, so it didn't have to be extravagant, right?

My mom came into the kitchen, took one look at my work, and said, "Let's go." On the way back to the hobby store, she lectured me about treating women with respect and how she knew I could have spent more money on the mum and how I

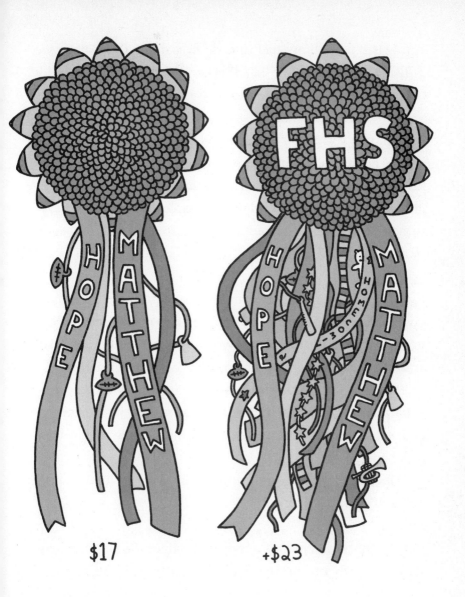

$17

+$23

had better not tell my dad that she was doing this. When we pulled into the parking lot, she handed me a twenty and a five and said, "You're going to do it right."

"Wow, thanks, Mom," I said.

"Thanks nothing. The twenty is from your jar."

We bought a bunch more ribbons, charms (including a little trumpet and a little clarinet), and all sorts of little thingies. And after my mom helped me staple, tie, and glue everything to the mum, it looked awesome. You know, for a gaudy bunch of fabric and plastic.

I MET UP WITH Hope before marching band practice on Friday to give her the mum. She pinned it on and was really excited about it. She gave me a garter-thing, which is like a mini-mum on an armband for boys to wear. It was only vaguely embarrassing.

"I'm imagining our secret alien overlords observing this ritual. They probably find it fascinating. Or just primitive and weird. Me give pretty sparkly thing. Female happy. Give arm band."

"One, you're in danger of ruining the moment. Two, thanks again. It's really beautiful."

MR. MURPHY WAS REALLY annoyed by all of the jangling bells and flowy ribbons on the field as we marched, but so many girls whined about the prospect of taking them off and wrecking them by leaving them on the muddy ground that he allowed it at practice. They wouldn't, however, be allowed on our uniforms at the game that night.

At one point, I saw the mum that Greg had made for Cindy from across the field. From about thirty yards away. As my section passed hers, I almost fell over in shock. You know how I mentioned that some mums have double mums? This thing had THREE. With a *mini teddy bear in the middle*. And the ribbons (had to be a hundred of them) dragged on the ground. It probably weighed twenty pounds! It wasn't pinned on her shirt—it had a strap that she wore around her neck. Jeez, Greg. Does your family own a satin factory?

THE HOMECOMING GAME wasn't awful. The weather was definitely better than earlier games, so instead of itchy and sweaty, the marching uniforms were merely itchy. We also had the halftime show down pretty well, so we didn't get yelled at afterward.

Since it was homecoming, there were little extras throughout the game. There was a crowning ceremony for the homecoming king and queen (no idea who either of them were), the oldest living alumni from Franklin (and maybe the world) were brought out, and some congressman conducted the band

for our über-rockin' version of "Play That Funky Music." He basically flailed his arms around for three minutes while we played the song without attempting to follow him.

After the game, the buses took us back to Franklin, and everybody either went home or changed clothes and headed to the homecoming dance in the gym.

Greg and I met Hope and Cindy in the hallway outside the band hall and headed over to the gym. We all had our homecoming junk on, and it jingled and clanged as we walked. The entrance to the dance was lined with balloon arches and draping ribbons. Cindy's mum got tangled up by the door, and she practically took out the whole display getting it unhooked. Classic.

"Not a word," said Greg.

Andrew was already inside with what my dad calls "the flavor of the week," so we joined them by some bleachers. Almost immediately, Cindy grabbed Greg and dragged him

to the dance floor. I almost passed out from the hilarity of watching her make him "dance." He looked like a Lego man. No elbows, no knees. Just sort of bobbing and rocking. Every once in a while he'd take a ribbon or charm from Cindy's mum right to the face. It was too much.

Just when I was sure I'd pee my pants or throw up from laughing too hard, Hope leaned in and said, "Let's dance."

A slow song was just starting, and I knew I could handle that. So I took her hand and led her over next to Greg and Cindy.

"I don't know if we can be friends after that display, Gregory."

"Eat it."

After the slow dance, which, let's face it, is basically like a hug that sort of sways, another fast one started. I made a move to head back to the bleachers, but Hope said, "I don't think so," and pulled me back. Dang it.

I had no choice. I started dancing. Remembering what I had just seen and not wanting to resemble it, I tried to make sure everything was bending a little bit. And Greg just stood there smiling and staring. I know I looked awkward. I heard Andrew yell, "BAH HA HA!" from the bleachers. Friends.

Finally, Cindy tugged on Greg's arm to get him dancing

again. And then, I guess things loosened up a bit. Within an hour, we were all out there—even Andrew, who rapped along with every hip-hop song the DJ played. He went from person to person getting right in our faces to make sure that *we all knew* that he knew the words.

A LITTLE BIT BEFORE 10, we were all pretty tired from dancing, so we took a break. I asked Hope if she wanted to go for a walk around the school.

"You guys are pretty good dancers," she said as we left the building.

"You, too. But then again, you're classically trained."

Hope winced. "I wish my parents would take those photos down. They're so cheesy."

"No, they're not," I said. "Listen. I've got a secret. The guys don't even know about this."

"Ooh, what?"

"My sister was in ballet growing up, and one year, for *The Nutcracker*, they were really short on 'party boys' for the beginning, so . . ."

"No."

"Yeah, it's true. It was in second grade. Look, Hope. I wasn't always so stinking cool. Nobody was, I guess."

"Matt. You're kidding me, right?"

"No, I'm serious. I was kind of a dweeb. My mom dressed me like a little choirboy. Greg had it worse, though, I guess. He had a flat top and wore sweats to school until just a couple of years ago, and Adam—"

She grabbed me with both hands. Her eyes were wide. "Matt. Back up. *The Nutcracker*. I was in *The Nutcracker* for five years straight. Through most of elementary school. I think I was a mouse in second grade. We were in a ballet together!"

"Whoa!" I yelled. "That's so awesome that it's a shame we can't tell ANYBODY EVER."

A loud voice behind us cut through our laughter. "No outside privileges."

That killed the moment like a punch to the stomach. I turned to see a mammoth of a parent chaperone. "I'm sorry?" I asked.

"Either inside the gym or off of school property," he said. "No outside privileges."

Outside privileges? It was like he'd glanced at a chaperone script and was remembering it all wrong. I didn't want things to escalate. He didn't seem to be the type to take things lightly. "Sorry. We're heading inside."

I tried to not be in a crappy mood after that, but it was tough.

THE NEXT MORNING, I woke up thinking that I needed a plan of action. I really liked Hope, but if I wanted to save any money at all for drums and still be able to go on dates, I needed to get creative. I made a list of cheap and free dates.

I knew I'd still get roped into expensive stuff like going to movies and

restaurants, especially for double dates, but I could pretty easily save up for a used drum kit by keeping costs down as much as possible.

- Watching a movie at home (free rentals at the library)
- Picnic in the park (with food from home)
- Free day at the museum
- Art walk (all of the galleries and art studios are open and have SNACKS)
- Thrift store shopping
- Bike ride
- Board games at a coffee shop
- High school and college theater shows

One of the first of the cheap dates we went on was a picnic. I made sandwiches at home and packed them in my bag. It was absolutely free, and she really liked it. Dating is easy.

I packed a couple extra pieces of bread to feed the ducks. Hope is really into birds.

"Actually, it's not a great idea to feed bread to the birds," she said.

"What?" I asked. *Oh, crap. Did I just ruin the date?*

"It's not poisonous or anything. It's just not part of their natural diet, and it makes them dependent on people."

"Good company, great sandwiches, *and* a lesson in wildlife preservation," I quipped. The ducks around us watched for signs of a handout. Sorry, birds. Bugs and minnows are on the menu tonight.

"I can't wait until the Canada geese come back," she said. "They're my favorite."

"Yeah, they're so tough. One of them bit my sister last year. It was awesome."

"I think they're majestic."

"—right on the back of the knee. She was screaming and crying. I'll never forget it. Too cool."

FISH TACO, BURRITO, STUFFING

A couple of months later, my drum fund was back to zero.
For starters, I had been fired from/quit my job well
before the end of my second pay period. I went in for an evening shift on a school night, but a hostess had written down
the wrong time on my schedule, so I was thirty minutes late.
Kyle called me into his office, where he started hassling and
lecturing me about responsibility and how I was letting him
down and my mom down and the staff down. Letting my
mom down? What?

"This is a family business. How does it look when some-one in the family acts as if the rules don't apply? It makes all of us look bad. If there is special treatment—"

I had to interrupt. "I already told you that the time was wrong on my schedule. What do you want me to do?"

It didn't matter. He kept rattling on.

"You have duties and responsibilities as an employee at this restaurant to . . ." Blah, blah, blah. . . .

Finally I just threw my hands up and yelled, "Well, maybe this whole thing wasn't such a good idea!"

He jumped out of his chair. "GOOD! LEAVE!"

I started walking out the door, and then I turned to face him again. If I had known how to rip my Pepe's shirt off pro-wrestler-style (and if I wasn't kind of awkward about being shirtless in public) I totally would have gone for it. RRRAAAAAA!!! Instead, I said, "You should really work on your people skills."

"I WILL! THANK YOU!"

My uncle, the giant toddler.

The day after that, my mom handed me an envelope with

Pepe's letterhead containing $36 cash. It was what I had earned in that period. She also gave me her speech about quitting things. It all goes back to her letting me quit soccer, you know.

So I was back to depending on my allowance.

I STILL MANAGED to be a decent boyfriend, go to shows, and basically to coast in a state of near-bankruptcy. A bad burrito even elevated me in the indie scene echelon. This older kid, Jacob, usually ran the door when shows were at the mini-golf place (as they most often were since Gino's went south), and one night, when Hope and I got there early, I saw him slouching on a stool and clutching his gut.

"You all right?"

"What's your name?"

"Matthew," I said. "Matt."

"Matt. Watch the door real quick. I gotta take care of some business."

So for about fifteen minutes, I collected door money as people trickled in. Sully was a little taken aback when he saw me. He paused for a second, punched my arm and said, "Way to go, kid." He made a move to walk past me, but I put my arm up to block him.

"Five bucks," I said.

"The power went to your head real quick, didn't it?"

Then Jacob, ghost-faced and shaking, came back.

"Jeez, Jacob. You look like hell on rye," said Sully.

Jacob smiled and lifted a clenched fist, then dropped it to his side. "I'm too tore up to smash your face in today, buddy." Then he turned to me. "I'm going home. Half of the money is for the touring bands, and the other half goes to the door. You got this?"

"I . . . yeah, man. Are you going to make it?"

"Burrito," he grunted.

So even though I was stuck at the back and couldn't see everything, I was helping run things. Scene point EXPLOSION. At the end of the night, I split half of the money up with the touring bands and gave the mini-golf manager the other half.

"I told that boy to lay off the convenience store cuisine," he said.

At the next show, Jacob hopped off his stool when he saw me. "Matt. Take the reins." He handed me a small stack of bills and disappeared into the crowd. So I kind of had a function. I was PART OF IT and more determined than ever to start a band.

I started hanging out a little bit with these two guys, Shane and Darren, and we even talked some about playing music together. Nothing major. Darren had a keyboard and a small amp, but that was it.

Shane's a weird kid. He always wears cardigans or corduroy jackets and button-up shirts and old-timey pants, and he keeps his hair neatly combed. But we like a lot of the same music. The kid just fell through a time warp somewhere along the way. He would always say in his quiet, articulate voice, "I'm asking for an electric guitar for Christmas." He had a baritone ukulele, which he assured us was basically the same thing. So he already knew how to play guitar. Power chords at least.

Then Darren, Shane's opposite in dress and volume, would shout, "Yeah! Then Matt gets drums and we're in business." Simple. That was a typical exchange. Then we'd discuss what type of music we'd play and what we'd be called. Then it would trail off into talking about bands we like, and since I didn't have drums and Shane didn't have a guitar, there was no use in getting serious.

It was definitely cool to have friends who were into music. I mean, Greg was dragged to shows with Cindy every once in a while, and Hope usually came to shows, too. Even Andrew and Adam came a couple of times when the shows happened at the mini-golf place, but those guys weren't really into it. Darren and Shane loved music like I did, and it was great to talk about something besides marching band and *Guilds of Destiny*.

BETH CAME HOME for Thanksgiving and she spent two days doing laundry. Apparently there aren't washing machines in Oklahoma. She cluttered up the hallway with her dirty clothes, and my parents didn't say a *word*. I get berated for leaving a T-shirt on the bathroom floor, but Beth can create—let's just call it what it is—a (smelly) *fire hazard*, and The Man lets it slide. It's a personal vendetta.

I was drumming in my room on Thursday morning along

Secret tattoo. I'm waiting for the perfect blackmail opportunity.

dramatic bangs

Two voice modes: one to sweet-talk, one to give orders.

Beth

to *Sendak Sendak* and feeling pretty good about my improving skills (I was probably the best electronic plastic toy drummer in the neighborhood), when I heard a knock on the door through the music. I looked up to see my grandparents.

"Hello, Matthew!"

I got up and gave them a hug. "Hey, hey, hey."

"So what cha doing there?" asked my grandmother.

"Oh, I'm working on my drumming. I'm saving up for a drum set."

"I thought he was a trumpet player," said my grandfather.

"Yeah, for school," I replied. "This is for outside of school."

"All right. If you say so. But you should probably get good

at one instrument instead of spreading out and being mediocre at multiple ones."

"Ah."

"Your father was a hell of a trumpet player as I recall,"
said my grandmother.

"Yeah, he's never missed an opportunity to remind me."

"Matt, come show your grandfather how to work the
remote."

AT DINNER, BETH had wine with my parents and grandparents. How fancy. How grown up. As they discussed the
vintage of their pee-no gree-jee-oh, I noted the subtle cran-
berry and apple undertones in my cran-apple juice. Ah. Lovely
bouquet.

And what conversation. My
grandparents went down the list
of who had died, details about
the new manager of their local
grocery store, and what some of
my dad's old classmates were up
to. Riveting.

Beth has this way of saying
something really snotty with
her eyebrows raised and then

taking a sip of her drink for added snootiness. Something like, "Well, you *know* she got pregnant at church camp," (brows up, sip). Ugh. Brutal. I couldn't wait to get out of the house. Now that football season was over (our hometown heroes didn't make the playoffs), I had a long, open weekend ahead of me, and I wanted to use it.

SHANE AND DARREN and I hung out all day on Saturday. We went to the music store to check out equipment. Shane started to play a guitar that cost more than his house, but he got the eye from an employee, so he traded waaaay down to a beat-up junker guitar to goof around on. Darren fell in love with a vintage home organ with colorful buttons and levers, warbly sounds, and switches for little bossa nova beats.

I made my way to the percussion section and sat down at a drum set with faux wood finish. I picked up a pair of drumsticks and hit a real snare drum for the first time. It was loud, jarring, and intense. The drumhead hit back against the stick. The hard plastic of my toy drums didn't have bounce like that. It was a completely different experience. Next, I hit a cymbal. WHOA. It shook the room. I hit each of the toms once, then looked down at my feet. I had completely forgotten about the kick drum pedal. In my bedroom practicing, it never occurred to me since I had the "bass drum" pad on my toy kit. Real drums would change everything.

I thought of a beat that I had played a thousand times before and tried it out. I ignored the kick drum and used just the high hat, a low tom, and the snare drum. It wasn't completely dreadful.

"She's a beauty of a kit." A bearded figure was standing next to me. I recognized him from the commercials the store ran around Christmas. "Good for beginners." Was it that obvious?

"Yeah," I said. "I'm kind of in the market for something like this."

"That kit there is a heck of a deal. $799. Down from $1299. Drums, cymbals, hardware. I'd even throw in the stool." That was almost three times what I intended to spend and well over ten times more than I currently had.

"Thanks," I said. "I'll give it some thought." He shot me a smile that had a *yeah, right* undertone, and he turned to find someone who wouldn't waste his time.

I watched him approach Darren. "She's a beauty of an organ."

ONE GIANT LEAP

O n Monday, as Hope and I were leaving our history class and heading to lunch, a poster caught my eye. There was an angled photo of a band in the midst of a formulaic "rock out" moment. "Hey, I'll catch up," I told Hope.

"O . . . kay," she said. "I'll save you a seat."

I approached the poster. In bold, tattered letters, the headline said "BATTLE OF THE BANDS." The layout and glossy production quality of the poster suggested that it wasn't a

4th annual ROCK106
BATTLE OF THE BANDS
all ages and genres welcome
CASH PRIZES!

Show starts at 6pm on Fri...
Civic Center in downtown...
enter your band by Dec 15th at www.ro...

ROCK106
HOLY CRAP!

Henson
Music
Center

JAGUAR
CREAM
EXPLOSIVE ENERG...
RRRRRRAAAAAA...

4th annual ROCK106
BATTLE

06
BANDS
OF THE
all ages and genres welcome
CASH PRIZES!

typical punk show. There were rarely posters for those—not printed ones, anyway. This thing had some cash and corporate sponsorship behind it. There were little logos all along the bottom: a radio station, a music store, an energy drink, and a couple of others. Under the headline, it read "all genres and ages welcome." It was scheduled for a Friday in late January at the civic center auditorium.

I stared at it for a minute or so before heading to the cafeteria. I saw Sully poking at his lunch at a table near the entrance, and I asked him what he thought of the whole battle of the bands thing.

"Meh. . . . Battles of the bands are pretty lame. I mean, cash prizes are cool. I guess if you just overlook the whole contest part of it and just think of it as a show, they can be all right. If good bands enter. You gotta wade through some real crap, though."

"Cool. I'll let you get back to your guts and sawdust sandwich."

Sully threw his burger at the wall. "This food is *ASS*." As he got dragged away by an assistant principal, I decided to take a big plunge. I went back to the battle of the bands poster, wrote down the Web address, went to the library, got on the Web site, and signed up.

Band: **Manhassler**

Genre: **Post-apocalyptic**

Contact: **Matthew Swanbeck**

All right. The hard part was taken care of. All that was left was, let's see, a drum kit, other band members, a song, and . . . um, everything. All that was left was everything.

PA RUM PA PUM PUM PUM

A couple of weeks later, I received an email about the battle of the bands. No auditions, no request for a recording. Just a message of congratulations. For what, exactly? Entering my email address correctly? Anyway, I was in.

For the rest of the month, I tried to put the battle of the bands on hold and focus on willing my drum kit into existence. My mom left some Oprah book in the bathroom about positive thinking, and I decided to give it a shot. Shane and Darren joined my "band," and wanted to practice. I held them at bay and assured them that my parents would come around, and I'd get a drum kit for Christmas. And *then* we could practice.

In case I couldn't will my drums into being, I had managed to save $65 between allowance and selling more CDs. Yeah, I got rid of some good stuff. I put most of it on my computer, which is maybe illegal or at least unethical, but the situation was pretty critical. And my grandparents usually gave me *some* money at Christmas, so I could probably buy a bottom-of-the-line kit.

The problem was, I knew I had to buy Hope a present. Sully told me I should break up with her. His advice was, "You should always dump a girl in November and not get back with her or another girl until after Valentine's Day. And if her birthday is between November and February, you're

golden." It almost made sense, but then I realized that I had never really seen Sully with a girl. I decided to go for a budget present.

Hope and I planned to exchange gifts on the twenty-first, because her family was going to Colorado for Christmas and New

Year's. I found some cute (I guess) earrings at one of those girl stores in the mall: a pair of red wooden fish. Only six dollars. And they were hand-painted. By someone who paints about a thousand pairs a day, but hand-painted nonetheless.

As I was wrapping them in the comics page of the newspaper, I got a funny feeling. I gave Cindy a call. "So, Cindy, Christmas is coming up. Yeah, Hope and I are exchanging gifts in a couple of days. Yep. Christmas time . . . is . . . here. . . ."

"You want to know what she got you."

"No, no, no. I mean, I . . ."

"I'll say this. She got you something really thoughtful and awesome. So you better bring it. What did you get her?"

"Lemme call you back."

I got on my computer and scoured for something good. *Think,* Matt. *Think: thoughtful, fast.*

Suddenly it hit me—the perfect idea. I searched . . . JACKPOT! A sterling silver Canada goose necklace. Just the thing for her. Eighteen bucks. Not bad! And overnight shipping was only . . . twenty-two dollars. Ass.

I looked over at the cheap earrings sitting in the middle of the wrinkled comics page.

"BETH!"

I put up with Beth teasing me and calling me "lover boy"

for five minutes, and she finally let me give her the cash and use her debit card to buy the necklace. She was going to charge me an additional 15 percent "convenience fee," but I told her that Mom probably wouldn't be so happy about one of her children exploiting the other. Forty bucks later, I had a silver Canada goose necklace coming my way. Boyfriend of the year. My parents would be getting drawings and coupons for extra chores. Maybe I'd play a Christmas carol on my trumpet. That's a guaranteed Tearful Mom Moment.

And I'd give the fish earrings to Beth.

HOPE CAME OVER to do the gift exchange, and while our moms talked in the kitchen, we sat on the couch. She handed me a book-sized package. "You first."

I pulled off the wrapping paper and held a hardbound book in my hands. It didn't have a title on the cover or spine. I opened it up. Blank paper. And not regular paper. Creamy, thick art paper with soft edges. Nicer than anything I had used before.

"I . . . this is . . . this is *great*," I said. It really was. I just stared at it for a minute and felt the sides of the pages.

"It's good for pencil, pen, even watercolor," she said. "Oh. Turn to the back."

I flipped to the end of the book. On the last page, there were two small photographs of young children. They had been zoomed and cropped, so they were a little grainy, but it only took me a second to realize what they were. One was Hope dressed as a soldier with mouse ears, and the other was of me amid a group of boys dressed in suits with short pants. Pictures from *The Nutcracker.*

"I can't believe it. Thank you so much." I must have stared at it for *another* two minutes before I snapped out of it. "Right. Sorry. Here. Merry Christmas."

I wondered if my gift to her was even close to what she gave me in comparison.

"A Canada goose!" She jumped off the couch and did a little

dance. "Help me get it on!"

She sat down in front of me and pulled her hair up. I saw our moms poke their heads around the corner to see. I felt weird touching Hope in front of her mother, but she smiled.

A few minutes later, Dr. Garcia came into the room. "Hope, honey, I have to go to the office for a few hours, so we're going to have to get going."

I sent my mom a telepathic message. She received it. "Maria, if the kids want to watch a movie and have dinner here, I can take Hope home after."

"Sounds great. See you at home, hon."

Hope and I found a Christmas movie on TV, and she put

her head on my shoulder and wrapped her hand around her goose necklace. Not even my dad flashing me the double thumbs-up ruined the mood.

EARLY ON CHRISTMAS MORNING, I peeked out into the living room in hopes of seeing a drum kit–shaped present under the tree. I didn't see any boxes that I hadn't already shaken. Sweaters and books and slacks, no doubt. The Christmas stockings had some things in them, you know, from Santa (if you don't believe in him, HE WON'T COME), but I was pretty sure a drum kit wouldn't fit in there. That would be candy canes and art supplies and stuff like that. Probably a pair of socks.

My previous box-shaking had left me with few surprises. I got to guess what *color* the sweater was. And what particular books I got. And, oh, corduroys—not jeans. Corduroys. Unfortunately, my grandparents went light on the cash ($30) and heavy on the clothes.

As I was flipping through my new books, I heard my dad say, "One more thing for you, Matt." It was the crappy gift fake-out! They got me drums!

I turned around, and my dad was holding an unwrapped cardboard box. He set it down in front of me and put on his proud-dad face. I opened the box, and inside was a snare drum and a little metal stand.

"Thought that could get you started."

"Oh . . . thanks, Dad."

"Figured that if you were really going to get some drums, you needed a proverbial kick in the pants. Or at least something more real than a toy to see if you're really interested. And if you're not, I can take it back to the pawnshop and get my gun back. Or, most likely, a new gun."

"You traded a gun for this?"

"Your old man has a hundred guns."

"Thanks, Dad. This is really cool." And I meant it.

"There's another part in the box."

I pulled the drum out of the box, and underneath was a black rubber practice pad.

"When I'm home, use that."

"No problem."

"For the record, my position on the best choice of instrument stands. But if you insist on giving yourself an equipment handicap, I suppose you'll have to rely on your father-given good looks to keep the good-looking women away from the trumpet player."

AFTER I HAD TRIED ON all of my super keen Christmas clothes and we had a family lunch, my grandparents drove home, and I took my snare drum into my room. I set up the stand and put on the practice pad. I played along to some music using my earbud/headphones method.

Suddenly, I had an idea. "Beth?"

No answer.

"She went to a movie with Kim!" called my mom. On Christmas Day. Shame on her.

Even though she went to college hours away and lived in a dorm there, my sister's room at home was an untouched shrine. I opened her door and peeked around. In the corner, under a stack of books and stuffed animals, was what I was looking for.

Beth had gone through a karaoke phase in high school, and my dad had given her a home system for a birthday. It was most likely from a pawnshop, since it sported dual cassette decks, a single 15-inch speaker, and no TV screen or anything for lyrics. It was all the best the mid-nineties had to offer. She had used it a few times to show gratitude, and then it became a shelf.

I carefully unstacked everything, removed the system, and stacked everything up the way it was before, now just two feet lower. There was so much junk in the room that there was no way she'd even notice it was missing.

I called Darren, and he came over with the missing pieces:

a quarter-inch cable and an eighth-inch to quarter-inch adapter. With that, I could go from the toy drum's headphone jack to one of the microphone inputs on the karaoke machine.

When amplified, the electronic "drum" sounds were still a bit silly, but they were a lot more substantial and crunchy than they were in headphones. Especially with the reverb knob turned up halfway.

"I don't know, man," said Darren. "That actually sounds pretty awesome. Shane got a guitar and amp for Christmas. Maybe we could—"

"It's just for practice. I'm not giving up on this yet."

"Yeah, that's what I mean. We could get together and practice with this stuff and maybe go from there."

I didn't like how excited he was about the crappy toy sounds, but actually getting the band started sounded good. I could work on building a real kit while getting ready for the battle of the bands. After all, it was only a few weeks away.

THE GATHERING

It snows about twice a year in my town, and it usually
doesn't stick. Sometimes we get lucky, though, and just before New Year's, we got about three inches. And when that
happens here, it's a Muddy Winter Wonderland: dirty snow-
men in every yard, forts that are half snow, half leaves and
grass.

Andrew, Adam, and I walked over to Franklin after we
got the word online that a snow war was in the works. Greg
was probably picking out baby names with Cindy. When we

arrived, there were already about fifteen people, mostly band dorks, building forts and mini-bunkers in the practice field. One kid ingeniously brought a wheelbarrow from home, and he was hauling in snow from the other side of the school. Hey, limited resources.

We split up and immediately started pelting each other. It wasn't long before the snow started wearing out, and the increasingly muddy snowballs upped the stakes. When hit, it went from "Hahahaha!" to "Oh, gross!" to "That's it—I'm done."

Andrew and I were running from Adam, and we ducked for cover behind the band hall dumpster. There I found a discarded marching band cymbal. It had a three-inch crack, but when I held it by the strap and hit it against the dumpster, it crashed. Kind of tinny and messed up, but it made a cymbal-ish sound.

Suddenly, I felt something cold and wet smash into the side of my face. I had a mouth full of icy sludge and decomposing grass. Sick. Adam had ambushed us. I deflected his second slush ball with the cymbal and ran back to the field, where things were a lot calmer. Half of the group had left, and the others were walking around, kicking down the forts, and making dirty sculptures. Dirty in both material and theme. I prayed that they'd last until school started back

TEXAS SNOWBALL

30% snow, 20% slush, 15% ice, 15% plant matter, 10% mud, 10% other

up, but I knew they'd be gone in a few days.

I scoured a few pawn shops and thrift stores for a cheap cymbal stand, but apparently all of the available drum parts in town had been scooped up, no doubt by parents who love their children.

My last hope was a flea market across town. It took me twenty minutes to bike there, and there wasn't a cymbal stand, or drum parts or hardware of any kind. Well, I *did* find a little tambourine adorned with a cartoon drawing of Jesus and a lamb.

Then, as I was walking a final lap through the store, I noticed a weird floor lamp that had three adjustable arms with bulbs on two of the ends. The third arm was missing the bulb and little lampshade, and the main bar had a couple of dings in it. The electrical cord also had some chew marks—either from a dog or a baby. The price tag said "$8—as is."

I took my finds up to the register, and a gentleman with

faded blue tattoos all over his arms (honestly, I couldn't make out a single picture or word) started to ring me up. On the floor by the checkout table, there was a greasy box full of barbed-wire pieces and assorted rusty metal things. Sitting in the middle was a cowbell. Not a cowbell like you'd see attached to a hair metal drum kit, but like, an actual cow's bell—with the little bar in the middle to make it clang.

"What's the double-secret back door price on this?" I asked, using one of my dad's best pawn shop lines.

"Hell, just take it."

WHEN I GOT HOME, I laid everything out in the middle of my room. I duct-taped the cymbal strap to the arm of the lamp that didn't have a bulb or lampshade and bent it so it hung free. I took one of the bulbs and shades off and taped the cow bell (with the little clapper removed) to the end of the arm. I started to remove the bulb from the third arm, but realized that I hadn't checked to see if the "as-is" lamp actually worked. I mean, I was going to use it as a stand for drum stuff, not a lamp. But just to check.

To be safe, I got some electrical tape from the garage and covered all of the exposed wire. Then I plugged it in, hit the switch, and the remaining bulb came on. The little plastic lampshade made the light green. Nice touch.

So instead of attaching the tambourine to the third arm, I decided to leave the bulb and shade on. I adjusted the cowbell so that arm could share with the tambourine. Finally, I taped over the empty bulb sockets.

I arranged my practice kit. The electronic drum toy sat on top of the karaoke machine that amplified it. That sat on top of the side of the base of the lamp to secure it. On the other side of the lamp, I put the snare drum.

I connected the lamp and karaoke machine to an extension cord with two inputs and plugged it in. I turned off my bedroom lights, and the room glowed green from my . . . drum kit? No, just my practice kit.

I played for two hours before calling Darren. "It's time to practice."

"YES. YES. Okay. I'm calling Shane. My house—tomorrow at three. YES."

GETTING MY PRACTICE kit to Darren's the next day was tricky. My parents were already back at work, and Beth was back in Oklahoma. Sully's car was still spread out all over his driveway. So I was on my own. I put everything inside a 55-gallon plastic trashcan that was in the garage, and put that on top of my skateboard. Then I rolled my stuff twenty blocks to Darren's house in the freezing cold. Rock and roll isn't all glamour. It's hard work, too.

I FINISHED SETTING EVERY-thing up in Darren's rumpus room just as Shane showed up.

"Whoa."

"I know!" exclaimed Darren. "It's rad, right?"

"It's just for practice. Obviously. I'm thinking that maybe I can borrow a kit for the show," I said.

I can't do an ollie, so I use it to hauly.

"Does all that stuff work?" asked Shane.

I plugged in the extension cord and played a sloppy beat.

Shane smiled broadly and spoke more loudly and with more authority than I've ever heard from him. "*That's* your kit. You're not borrowing anything."

"YES," added Darren.

Shane looked over at the trash can I brought everything in. "What's that for?"

"Oh, that's just for carrying it all around."

"Or, check this out." Shane flipped the can over and placed it next to the snare drum.

I hit the top (er, bottom) of the plastic bin and it made a dull tap.

"Hit the side," offered Darren.

THUD.

"It's like a kick drum!" shouted Darren.

"Settle down, kiddo," I said.

I walked around to the front of my drum kit. I remembered my dream kit drawing from a few months back. This was absolutely nothing like it. But something about it made sense.

The next four hours were pretty unproductive. The first half was making a bunch of noise and getting everybody's volumes right so we could hear everything. The second half was a slow wind-down of playing and a lot of talk about what we should go get to eat. We had one riff that sounded pretty good, but that's as far as we got. We decided we'd practice again the next day. And to go get sandwiches.

HOPE CAME BACK FROM Colorado the next day and immediately wanted to see me. I told her I had band practice and that maybe we could rent a movie in the evening or something. She was not happy about that.

"You've been in a band for one day and you've already dissed me. Let's not make this a pattern."

With that settled, I rushed over to Darren's house. As I leaned my bike against his garage door, I got a call from a number I didn't recognize.

"Hello?"

"Matt. Matt. It's Sully."

"Sully? Where are you calling me from?"

"A pay phone. Didn't want to use my cell. Listen. Where are you?"

I gave him Darren's address, and in less than ten minutes, there was a knock on the window. I lct Sully in through the back door, and he collapsed on the couch.

"Okay, listen. If anyone asks, I've been here for the past couple of hours."

"Whoa, whoa, whoa. What did you do?" I asked.

"I may or may not have been involved in a window-breaking incident. Just help me out."

We all looked at each other. Shane shrugged. Darren said, "All right. It's cool."

"Good. I owe you one."

See, when Sully said, "I owe you one," that's foreshadowing. So remember that for later.

While Sully helped himself to about a hundred cookies, fiddled with his cell phone, and slept on the couch, we got back to practicing.

Despite the crumb-covered oaf snoring in the background, we managed to come up with a song-writing system. Shane would come up with a simple chord progression on his guitar, and then Darren would find a melody to play with or just chords that matched. Then I'd put a beat on top of it. We came up with four or five different riffs that way. It would just be a matter of choosing some and putting them together.

I also managed to come up with an idea for a song about *Guilds of Destiny* addiction. I had two lines.

It's 12 steps to recovery
vs. 6 steps to my PC.

By then, it was getting late, so I woke Sully up and moved my stuff to a corner of the room.

"I'll give you a ride," Sully said as we started out the door. "And remember, I was there with you the whole time."

"Okay, no problem—HEY!"

Sully was reaching down and letting the air out of my back bicycle tire. "It's better for the story this way," he said. "I'll pump it back up before dropping you off."

When we pulled up to Sully's house, his dad stormed out the front door. "Where the hell have you been? The police came by. They think you broke some windows."

Sully pulled my bike out of the back of the truck. "What?

I've been with Matt. He got a flat on the way to band practice, so I drove him and then I hung out there."

"Why didn't you answer your phone?"

"Oh, shoot. Sorry, Pop. I didn't hear it ring. The band and all."

Sully's dad turned his gaze to me. "Matt?"

"Yes, sir?"

"Sully's been with you?"

"Yes, sir."

He kept his eyes on me for a good five seconds. He squinted, as if trying to pull any hidden truth out. I tried

my best to look sincere without looking like I was *trying* to look sincere. Finally, he said, "Okay. I'll call them back and let them know."

"Thanks, Pop. I don't know why they think I did that. That's weird. Hmm. Matt, let's check out your tire."

BAND VS. BAND

When school started up again, people were talking about the battle of the bands all over the place. There was a lineup posted on the Web site, and there were sixteen or seventeen bands on the list. Some bands that I had seen and knew were playing, but the majority of the schedule was made up of non-scene bands. Some singer-songwriter people, some lame hard rock bands, some middle-aged classic rock-types, a jazz ensemble, rappers.

So yeah, something for everybody, I guess. Musicians

seemed to be coming out of the woodwork. I saw a wanna-be heartthrob with an acoustic guitar wooing a group of girls with his whispery singing and side-swept bangs in the courtyard by the library (and they were totally falling for it). And there was another guy passing out little flyers for his dad's bar rock band. He wore a black T-shirt of the same band that featured an electric guitar in flames. Tuff. I took one of the fly-

7ENDER 5URRENDER
LIVE IN CONCERT AT THE
BATTLE OF THE BANDS!!!!
CIVIC CENTER FRIDAY JANUARY
HARD ROCK LIKE YOU'VE
NEVER SEEN BEFORE!!!!
TSHIRTS AND TANK TOPS
AVAILABLE 4 PURCHASE!!!!
THEY'LL BLOW THE ROOF OFF!

ers and said, "Oh, yeah. They're playing right after my band."

"What's your band?" he asked.

"Manhassler."

He studied me for a second. "What are you, hard rock? Heavy metal?"

"We're . . . I don't know. I hesitate to say indie rock, but . . . maybe." I might as well have said, "We play a mix of industrial mariachi and borbleeperflügen."

"Huh?"

Darren ran up to me in the hall and said, "We should record and put out a CD before the show." I reminded him that we needed to actually write a song and be able to play it first.

Since football season was over, we didn't have to have marching practice every morning before school. Just a couple times a week during first period because of competitions. The rest of the time, we'd be splitting into different bands for concert season.

Most of the freshmen automatically went into freshman band, unless you were good enough to bump up into either symphonic or honors band. After a chair test that I didn't practice for, I was put as third chair of freshman band. I felt like it was a good spot. Easier songs, and I didn't even have to play the harder first trumpet parts. Second trumpet parts in the easiest band—okay by me.

The bad part was that Andrew and Greg both placed into symphonic band, and Hope got into honors band. I made a mental note to give her extra attention and presents and stuff so she wouldn't ditch me for some schmoozing honors guy.

The day after classes resumed, Mr. Murphy made an announcement before splitting us up.

"Our first event of the semester is in mid-February, and to get a feel for the competition and for other concerts later on, we're going to have a small concert in a couple of weeks,"

A handful of nerds hissed a celebratory *yessss.*

Then he announced the date. It was the same Friday as the battle of the bands.

"Mr. Murphy?" Jaye, the senior drum major, had her hand raised.

"Yes, Ms. Bergwell?"

"The citywide battle of the bands is on the same night."

"So?"

By my count, that affected more than fifteen people or so in band. Later, in the hall, I overheard someone say, "I ain't going. I don't care if I fail." By the end of the day, I was told that at least one band had already dropped out of the battle.

What the hell?! This was my first chance to play a show, and I was PISSED. The Man had no idea what was important. If given the choice between school band and my REAL band, Mr. Murphy would be missing his third chair freshman trumpet player. Hope's advice was to write Mr. Murphy a letter, so I got out a piece of paper.

Murphy.

I can't believe this. Are you so clueless that you'd think anyone wants to play ~~your~~ some crap concert on the same night as battle of the bands? NOBODY CARES. It's almost as if you insist that everybody hates you. Do you WANT your house to get egged? Do you WANT half of band to quit? I can't even believe how much of a moron you are for doing this.

Signed,
You SUCK

I reread the letter, crumpled it up, and threw it away. Way too mean. He'd flip out on it for sure. Then I got out a second piece of paper.

Mr. Murphy,

I'm writing this to let you know

that, unless the concert is canceled or moved, I'm going to have to quit band. The battle of the bands is on the same night, and it's important to me. Being in a band is my future. And I don't mean school band. Lots of people feel the same way.

Matthew Swanbeck

Again, I reread the letter. I went back to the band hall and put it in the mailbox outside of his office. Wait. I snatched it back out and wadded up the note. Then I got a third piece of paper and sat down on a riser.

Mr. Murphy,
Like many of my classmates, I'm very excited

about concert season. I plan on being a professional musician, and learning about music theory, and honing my skills at my instrument is very important to me.

Unfortunately, there are two music events on the same night this month. For a while now, many of us have been preparing for a citywide "battle of the bands." There are over a dozen of us scheduled to play in various bands, and ~~dozens~~ more from our ranks have planned to attend. There is even a jazz ensemble made up entirely of members of the Franklin band. I've been especially looking forward to that.

I'm writing in hopes that there could be a reschedule of the concert, as it is mostly just a practice for competitions, and the "battle" has been scheduled for some time. I believe I can speak for many of us in saying that we would greatly appreciate it.

Thank you,
Matthew Swanbeck

Now *that* was a golden letter. A bit hammy, sure, but golden. I put it in the box and went to my next class.

"JUST DON'T GO TO the thing." It was lunchtime, and Shane was squirting about a quart of mayo on his who-knows casserole.

"It's mandatory. If I don't go, I fail."

"Twewwy-twoo!" muttered Darren through a complete mouthful of grapes. It was a new group record. He chewed, swallowed, reattached his jaw, and continued. "So quit then. Adam: Put down twenty-two."

Adam dutifully updated the stats in The Book of Records. "The grapes are small here."

"I don't think quitting band is an option," I said. "My parents would kill me. Let's just see what happens in the next week and keep getting ready for the show in the meantime."

Hope grabbed my arm. "Matt, you can't quit band. One,

136

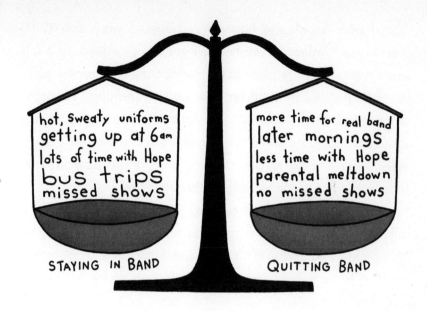

STAYING IN BAND	QUITTING BAND
hot, sweaty uniforms	more time for real band
getting up at 6am	later mornings
lots of time with Hope	less time with Hope
bus trips	parental meltdown
missed shows	no missed shows

that would be one less class we have together, and two, we wouldn't have the marching competitions and concerts together."

"But you'd have your *own* band, dude," said Shane.

Andrew jumped in. "This isn't the only concert your band can play."

"*Shows*, Andrew," I said. "They're called shows."

For the next few days, we practiced for the band concert in school, and Manhassler practiced for the battle of the bands (*show*) after school and hoped for things to work out. There was so much music in my brain, I got things mixed up a few times when I lost my place in the melodramatic Europe-y piece we were playing in band because I was humming "12 Steps" in my mind. The whole time, Mr. Murphy didn't say anything about my letter. I wanted *something*, even if it was me getting yelled at or a reaffirmation that the concert was happening as scheduled. The suspense was really getting to me.

And then, on Friday morning, just before we split up, it happened. Mr. Murphy tapped his conducting-stick-thing on his music stand and said, "Quick announcement. The concert is going to be moved from two weeks from today to the Friday after that."

He didn't even look at me.

"HMMM. YEAH, I GUESS maybe sometimes you have to play The Man's game to get your way." The Corvair was chugging black smoke into the air and bright green liquid onto the driveway. "Probably not the move I would've made. I can't stand sucking up to jerks like that."

"It wasn't so bad. I just wrote a short letter. I didn't have to say anything to him."

"Well, *good*," he whined, super-sarcastically. *"Now you can keep tooting your little trumpet."*

"See you later, Sully." No time for that. I had two weeks to eat, drink, and sleep the band.

Back home, I had close to thirty dollars and another letter to write.

Dear Hope,

I am writing to let you know that I am not going to be the best boyfriend for the next couple of weeks...

GETTING THERE

The letter to Hope, along with some daisies, went over pretty well. She knew how important the show was to me, and we scheduled out a few times to see each other—mostly dinner at her house or my house. So I basically got a free pass to practice all weekend and next, and every day after school until the show.

I didn't have to say a single word to Adam, Greg, and Andrew about not hanging out for a while. A new expansion pack had been released for *Guilds of Destiny*, so I wouldn't be missed at any cucumber sandwich brunches or afternoon garden parties or anything.

In that period, Manhassler probably spent as much time coming up with gimmicks and special effects for the show as we did practicing. You know those little party popper things with the strings that you pull to shoot out confetti and little streamers? Darren bought about fifty of them at a party supply store and we spent the better part of two afternoons building a contraption to pop them all at once. We made a

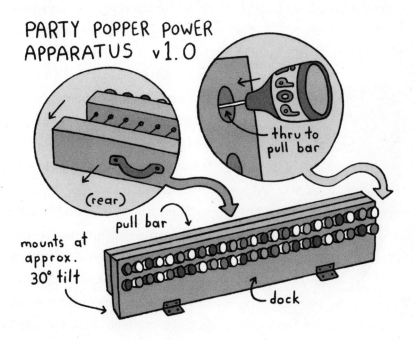

PARTY POPPER POWER
APPARATUS v1.0

(rear)

thru to
pull bar

pull bar

mounts at
approx.
30° tilt

dock

rack to house all of them in two rows. All of the strings were connected to a long bar that ran the length of the rack. The final product sat on top of his keyboard. The plan was for him to pull the bar at the show's climax, causing all of the party poppers to go off in the air, and hopefully on the crowd.

Shane completely covered the body of his guitar in a string of battery-powered twinkling Christmas lights. It took him a long time to wrap it so that the lights didn't cover any hardware or require any taping. It was a new guitar after all. In rehearsal, we found that after about fifteen minutes, the whole thing got really hot, but we were only playing one song at the show. Four or five minutes tops.

As for me, I painted an awesome medieval-style crest on my plastic trash can/kick drum. It had four sections: a fist, a sword, french fries, and a falcon. I know. Incredible.

Then we toyed with the idea of wearing costumes. Maybe gold capes and masks. Maybe as characters from *Guilds of Destiny*. We might have gone for it, but we realized that we were getting really short on time and decided to make sure that, you know, we could actually play our song.

A few days before the show, Hope called me all freaked out. She screamed, "I'm going to play in the battle of the bands!"

"You . . . what?"

"I just got a call from David. You know the jazz ensemble playing at the concert?"

"Uh-huh." I didn't correct her lame use of the word *concert*.

"Well, Kristen is the clarinet player, but she got mono, so they need a replacement!"

"Mono? That's great!"

I DON'T REMEMBER a single thing from any of my classes on the Friday of the battle of the bands. I could barely eat my goo at lunch. I kept running through the song in my head over and over, wondering if we were good enough. Wondering if *I* was good enough. Wondering if my *nontraditional* drum kit would get me laughed off the stage. I mean, only Shane and Darren had seen it. They loved it, but they're weird. Oh, crap. What would normal people think?

It seemed like the whole school was going to the show. It's almost impossible to get a decent show turnout most nights, but for something like this, people who otherwise have zero interest in music show up. Kind of like how church is completely packed on Christmas and Easter.

When the last bell rang, I bolted out the door and toward the bike racks. Darren and Shane and I planned to meet there and head to Darren's house together so we could get one last practice in before heading up to the show. When I got there, however, only Shane was waiting.

"Darren got detention," he said.

"What? What for?"

Shane sighed. "You know the buffalo head in the auditorium?"

Oh, no. "Yeah?"

"He flicked a bunch of pencils up there until he got some stuck—one on top and one right behind the ear. That one's actually pretty funny. Anyway, a teacher saw him."

"That's it?" I asked.

"Well, yeah, but they'll have to get a cherry picker in there to get them down. Point is, he's in detention for another hour."

"TODAY!" I yelled. "OF ALL FREAKING DAYS. We have to leave his house in less than two hours from now to go to the show! With travel time to his house and then to the venue . . . that gives us zero time to do a last-minute practice."

"We're done, man. We're done."

"Nah, not really," I said, trying to sound confident. "We've been playing nonstop for weeks. We're ready. This is just inconvenient."

Instead of standing around in the cold for an hour, we biked to Darren's house and rang the doorbell. His sister Michelle answered the door.

"What do you turds want?" she sneered, tugging at her poorly executed blond dreadlocks. Classy dame, that Michelle.

"We're here to practice and then go to the show. You're still driving us, right?"

"Since it's the only way I can use the wagon tonight, yeah. Where's my brother?"

"He's delayed," I replied. "Something about a buffalo."

"Jeez, you're weird," she said.

I eyed her henna-covered arms, giant ankh necklace, and trash bag–look-alike skirt. "Uh-huh. *I'm* weird."

Shane pulled his blazer collar over his nose and moved past her. "S'cuse us, milady." I followed. Yeah, Michelle kind of stinks. Not like B.O., really. Like hippie oils or sprays or whatever. I had a toy when I was a kid that smelled like her. It was a humanoid skunk. Anyway, that's my association. So yeah.

So while we waited for Darren, we ran through our song a few times, and then raided the kitchen. Shane heated up a frozen pizza pocket, but I decided that my nervous guts couldn't handle that kind of grease. I made a double-decker sandwich of lettuce, tomato, hummus, ketchup, crushed up corn chips, guacamole, this vegetarian bacon stuff, and a bunch of pepper.

"You better be staying out of my veggie bacon!" called Michelle from the living room.

"Like I'd even want that sick crap!" I yelled back.

When Darren finally arrived, we hurried to load up the car and pry Michelle away from her knitting so we could head to the venue.

"DO YOU KNOW why I stopped you, ma'am?" We hadn't even made it ten blocks before we got pulled over by a motorcycle cop.

"No, officer," croaked Michelle.

"Got yourself a brake light out."

"Oh, I didn't know. Thank you, sir." Sweating. In January.

"License and registration."

She trembled as she reached in the glove compartment and took out the insurance card. She handed it and her driver's license to the cop.

"I'll be back in just a bit." As soon as he started walking back to his motorcycle, Michelle started crying.

"Oh, crap. What did you do?" asked Darren.

"My license . . . got suspended a few weeks ago because I got too many stupid speeding tickets."

"You're so screwed!" yelled Darren. "Does Mom know?"

"No. I paid them. I figured everything would be fine. It's a 90-day suspension. I'm going to jail. Ohgodohgodohgod."

The policeman was back at the window. "I suppose you know that your license is suspended. Driving with a suspended license is a class B misdemeanor in the state of Texas, ma'am. This is serious business."

Michelle was really sobbing now. And I started thinking about getting to the show. I mean, yeah, the crying and jail time and all of that was sad, but this was my *first show*.

"I need you to step out of the car, please." WHOA. She was getting arrested! "You boys, too." Wait. What?

We all stepped out of the car. "You got a parent or guardian at home we can reach?"

"My mom . . . she's at work until seven." Michelle was

whimpering and slobbering all over herself. Her raccoon-like mascara was dripping down her cheeks. What a spectacle.

"All right. Here's what's going to happen. I'm giving you a ticket for the brake light, which is a helluva lot less than what you'd get if I went through with the driving with a suspended license."

"Thank . . . thank you . . ."

"And I can't have you driving, so you're going to have to leave your vehicle here and get a ride or walk to where you're headed." He really put the emphasis on the *VEE* in *vehicle*.

I gave Shane and Darren a "what-the-H-are-we-gonna-do" look. Shane took the lead. "Excuse me, Officer?" We were on our way downtown. See, our band is performing, and if Michelle can just drive us to—"

He handed the ticket to Michelle and then looked hard at Shane. "Son, I don't care if you were going downtown to put out a church fire. This young lady is not getting behind the wheel of this or any vehicle with a suspended license. You're going to have to figure something else out."

At that, some gibberish came over the policeman's radio, and he responded with some numbers and code words. Then he got back on his motorcycle and took off, leaving us standing on the curb.

"Screw this," said Darren. "Gimme the keys. I'll drive us."

"No way," I said, taking out my phone.

"Come on. You're the 'damn The Man' guy."

"Just wait a minute." I dialed and held the phone up to my ear. After a couple of rings, the other end picked up. "Sully," I said. "I'm calling in that favor."

SULLY HAD FINALLY BEATEN, duct taped, and black magic-ified his Corvair into driveable order, so he was less than thrilled that he couldn't drive it to the show and debut it as he had intended. That sporty little front-end trunk wouldn't hold all of our equipment. Especially with all of the extra bottles of various fluids to keep the car alive taking up most of the space. We needed The Beast.

"I don't know, kid. This is a pretty big favor. I've been working on that car for six months. The way I see it, now you owe *me* one."

"Fine. I owe you one."

THE COMPLETE, UTTER, AND AWESOME
DESTRUCTION OF HUMAN FACES

The battle of the bands was being held in the auditorium at the Civic Center. Really old-timey. It's probably the biggest building in town, wedding receptions, gun shows, Junior League Christmas festivals, plays, concerts—all at your local Civic Center! We were running a little bit late due to our ride mishap, and people were already being let in. The parking lot was filling up, but we got to go in through the back entrance to load everything in.

Sully grabbed Shane's amp as we got out of the truck.

"Hey, thanks, Sully," said Shane.

"Uh-huh."

The long-haired classic rock dude by the loading dock looked up from his clipboard. "Band?"

"We're Manhassler."

"Maaaaaaaaaaaan . . . hassler. Got it. You guys ready to ROCK?"

"RRRRRRAAAAAAA!!!" yelled Darren, metal fingers in the air. I winced in shame, and Darren suddenly looked uncertain. "I . . . was just trying to fit in. Yes. We are ready to rock if that is all right with you."

The rocker stamped our hands and waved us in. Once inside, Sully put the amp down and said, "Later, boys."

"Thanks for the ride, Sully," I said. "And the free admission you just scored was the one I owe you."

"Whatever. Hey, don't screw up so bad that I'm embarrassed to drive you home."

The backstage area was HUGE. The big, velvet curtain was shut, and musicians and technicians were rushing back and forth with gear. There were five or six men and women talking into headsets and making last-minute lighting changes and going over the lineup. It was way more professional-feeling than any show I'd been to. It was both thrilling and foreign. Jacob and the other guys who ran most of the shows at the mini-golf place sure as hell didn't have headsets or clipboards.

As we put our equipment in the holding area, I looked around: full stack amps; huge, beautiful drum kits. Then I looked back at our stuff: Darren's keyboard and little amp; my trash can of junk. There were guitars in *cases* that were nicer than Shane's guitar. And his amp looked like it was pooped out by some of the other amps in the room. What the hell were we doing?

"All right, dudes." Another classic rock guy was directing backstage traffic. "Once you're unloaded, you can head to the seating area. Come back to start setting up two sets before yours. We're alternating sets in front of and then behind the curtain for shorter breaks between bands. You'll set up behind the curtain while the previous performer is playing. So be quiet when you're doing that. When it's your time, you'll get a minute for a quick sound check, and then it's let'r'rip time."

We went through the side exit out into the auditorium. The door we came through said "Bands Only," and that felt really cool.

I spotted Hope, Cindy, Greg, Adam, and Andrew in the gathering crowd. We went to join them, and then I noticed my mom and dad farther back. They had found a little pack of other parents, including Hope's parents, to cling to.

I gave them a wave. "Great," I said to Hope. "Your parents are going to *love* me after hearing us play. We're playing a song about a video game. And you're playing in a classy jazz group."

"They *are* going to love it. It's going to be great!"

"We say 'cleavage,' Hope. *Cleavage.*"

"You know, for someone who's always going on and on about The Man, you sure care what they think about you."

THE MC WAS a local DJ. His voice definitely did not match his looks. It was weird hearing a smarmy radio voice coming out of a stumpy, bald guy in a Las Vegas–style button-up shirt. He gave a spiel about the variety of music at the show and the camaraderie of the local music scene (though the indie scene and the mainstreamy, bar-band scene didn't cross paths on any other night) and how, yes, it was a competition but everyone was a winner because we had such an amazing city (blah, blah, blah). Praise be to you, oh Noble Champion of the Musical Arts. And then he went on to explain the prizes: $1,000 for the top band, $250 for second place, and gift certificates for third.

Shane nudged me. "So do you think we have a chance at—"

"No," I said.

Manhassler was about eight bands in, so we got to watch the show with the audience for a while. There really was a variety of bands at the show. A crap-metal band, a pop-punk band that I'd seen a couple times, a really earnest Christian guitar-and-violin duo. When a country group was stepping out on stage, Hope grabbed me. "I gotta get ready!"

"You're going to do so great! I can't wait!" I said in my best supportive boyfriend tone. I really was excited for her, but I was mostly trying to keep myself from puking. The nerves. The *nerves*.

After a hip-hop group with dueling DJs finished and threw about twenty T-shirts into the crowd, the curtain lowered, and DJ Smarm came out and introduced Hope and the other jazz kids with, "Up next is a special treat. I don't think we've ever had a jazz band in the battle before. And these kids are all in high school. Ladies and gents, The Franklin Five!"

I'm not into jazz, like, at all, and I know I'm completely biased, but they were *amazing*. It was five minutes of crazy noodling and solos. Hope completely shredded. I knew she was a good clarinet player, but I had no idea she was that good. Kind of made me feel like a doofus. I mean, here was this honors band star who got ready for the show in like two

days. And she was with me—
third chair trumpet in the low-
est band at school, and a pretty
lousy drummer in a decidedly
mediocre whatever-we-were
band. Was it punk? Was it
power pop? Hell, I had no idea.

All I knew was that The
Franklin Five got a standing
ovation, and it was time for my band to head backstage to
start setting up.

Hope and I crossed paths in the loading area. "You were
so awesome!" I said.

"Oh, no, thanks. I mean, thanks. I kind of screwed up in
my solo."

"You're crazy. It was perfect. I'm really glad we don't have
to follow you guys."

"Thanks, Matt. Okay, I'll let you get ready. Break a leg! I
can't wait to hear you guys!"

I turned to my band. "Last chance to fake a seizure, gang,"
I said.

"HELL no! Let's melt this place!" yelled Darren, punching
the air.

There was a really phenomenal beardo metal band playing.

Their amps towered over them, and the parents in the crowd scowled from the time they started until the curtain closed in front of them.

"Hey, guys," I said, trying my best to sound like a badass. "Great job."

"Thanks, man. What's . . . that?" He was looking at my trash can.

"It's, um, my drums."

"Oh. Right on."

Once they cleared out their arena's worth of amps, we started loading our stuff in. It took all of two minutes, and once we were set up, it occurred to me that, while the previous band filled the whole area, we took up about a quarter of the stage. The backstage coordinator rushed over and whispered, "How many mics do you need?"

We had never practiced with microphones. We all just sang really loud simultaneously. "Um, three?"

"You got it, ace." And suddenly we each had a microphone in front of us for the first time.

Then he approached my drums. "Um . . . how should I . . . mic . . . these?" He looked completely puzzled.

"I guess we don't need to? Maybe?"

"You're the boss. I . . . okay." He left a microphone on a stand pointing toward the middle of my kit and ran offstage.

In front of the curtain, a singer-songwriter was whining and swooning about butterflies and constellations and love lost. We stood in our positions staring straight ahead. Then . . . applause. The MC made a couple of quick remarks to segue into the next band (US!) and then the curtain squeaked open.

Months of saving, spending what I had saved, and scheming had led to this. I looked back on every hassle, roadblock, and hang up, and a feeling of accomplishment and confidence surged through me. It lasted about half a second. The light hit my face and the good feelings splashed into my stomach.

I squinted through the spotlights and looked out at the silhouettes of the crowd. The auditorium was almost completely packed. I could just make out my friends, and a little farther back, the cluster of parents. The rest of the faces were a mix of people from school, people I recognized from shows, and a *whooooole* bunch of strangers. The clapping from our introduction died down, and there was a smothering two seconds of silence.

We were given quick little orders to check the microphones and play a couple notes. We each said, "Check!" Darren hit a couple of keys, and Shane strummed a chord. I hit the power strip to my karaoke amp and lamp. The crowd laughed as the light bulb came on. I hit the pads one time each, and there was a little more laughing. And whispering. Humiliating.

"We're ready if you are," came the voice in the PA.

"Okay, team," I said, looking at my crew.

Shane smiled, switched on the twinkling lights on his guitar, and hit the opening chord. There was no turning back.

These woods are dark!
I've got my crossbow!
Who goes there? Hark!
Here comes the death blow!

It's 12 steps to recovery
vs. 6 steps to my PC.

This room is dark!
Hey, where'd the sun go?
I've lost my teenhood
But should I stop? No!

It's 12 steps to recovery
vs. 6 steps to my PC.
The real world's too dull for me.
I live for Guilds of Destiny.

Goblins!
Spells!
Gauntlets!
Hit points!

Trolls!
Elves!
Swords!
Cleavage!

It's 12 steps to recovery
vs. 6 steps to my PC.
I'll take my chances 'cross the Lantys Sea
My guild's my family and my destiny
It's 12 steps to recovery
vs. 6 steps to my PC.
It's 12 steps to recovery
vs. 6 steps to my PC.

It's 12 steps to recovery
vs. 6 steps to MYYYYY PEEEEEE CEEEEE!!!!!

And with the final shouted line, Darren pulled the bar on the party poppers. They went off in the air, but not as spectacularly as we had originally envisioned. Shane strummed faster

and faster and threw himself on top of his amp and let the feedback build. I beat the hell out of my cymbal and then released the trick up my sleeve.

While the other guys were winding the song down into a mushy, screeching conclusion, I flipped the trashcan back over and loaded everything back into it. I gave a bow and pulled

it offstage while the others continued to wail and flip out. So much for the drummer being the last to leave, eh, Dad?

And then something really unexpected happened: Applause. Cheering, even. I ran back out on stage and soaked it in. I mean, I really soaked it in. Another deeeep bow.

Then the curtain closed in front of us. It was all over in less than four minutes.

So you're probably expecting the big TV ending. Sorry to disappoint. We didn't get carried on the crowd's shoulders down the aisle. I didn't look out and see Mr. Murphy giving me an understanding thumbs-up from the back of the auditorium. We didn't close the show in a glorious, triumphant moment. There were six or seven bands after us. We put our stuff back in the loading area and went back to watch the rest of the show with the crowd. And no, we didn't win. We didn't even place. Hope's ensemble, however, got third. So to top it off, hey, *this* drummer left with a good-looking woman. A prize-winning woman. God, that sounds sexist and horrible.

My parents caught up to us in the parking lot as we were loading our things back into the truck. "You were terrific, Matthew!" exclaimed my mother. "I could have done without the screaming and violence, but we're very proud. Of you, too, Hope. You are a very gifted musician."

"Thank you, Mrs. Swanbeck."

"You're a strange one, son-of-mine," said my dad. "I especially liked how you beat the rest of the band off stage. Way to stick it to your old man."

"You noticed that, eh? That was my dedication to you."

"Very clever. So are you going to save up for a kick drum or some toms now?"

"I don't know," I said. "My drums are kind of growing on me." I looked down at my kit. Less than two hours ago, I saw a trash can full of junk, but in a completely unplanned way, I had made things happen for myself. Damn The Man. Or something.

Adam and Andrew came over. "You guys were ROBBED!" yelled Andrew. "I was crapping my pants at your song." He ran off to hit on somebody, and Adam looked around at our equipment.

"So, do you think that maybe I could . . . join the band?"

Shane nodded. "We could actually really use a bass player."

"Yeah, that would be rad," I agreed.

"And you're crazy tall, which fits the stereotype," added Darren.

Adam smiled. "Sweet."

Sully drove all of us to Darren's house to drop off our

equipment. "Not bad, kid." That's all he said about our performance. And I know how hard it was for him to say something nice, so I took it as a high compliment.

I invited Sully to come get pizza with us, but he said he had a party to go to, and he added, "You couldn't pay me to eat that garbage." Hey, I still think it's good. So he took off, and Darren's mom drove us in the wagon with the busted brake light. I guess Michelle hadn't told her mom about the ticket and near-arrest yet.

As Greg and Cindy made out behind us, I looked over at Hope. "Say, I don't suppose any of those gift certificates you won tonight are for Gino's?"

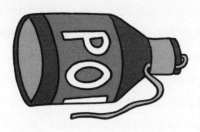

ONE OF THOSE EPILOGUE THINGS. YOU KNOW, A SHORT CHAPTER AT THE END WHERE THE READER DISCOVERS THE FATE OF THE PEOPLE IN THE STORY, USUALLY WITH A QUIP OR LINE THAT TIES IT ALL TOGETHER.

In early February, EverybodyLiveForever (formerly Manhassler) was booked to open for a couple of touring bands from Ohio at a coffee shop downtown. We had five songs and a pretty impressive light and pyrotechnic show—sparklers, a strobe, several chains of twinkling lights, and, of course, party poppers. I still had the same drum kit, but I had added some bongos that Darren got from his sister. He had traded/ blackmailed them for keeping the tail light incident a secret. On the night of the show, Greg, who had signed on as an unofficial "effects coordinator," was getting some dry ice ready, and I was taking money at the door. Adam approached and handed me five bucks to get in.

"We've got a problem," he said.

"Hold on." I asked Hope to take over for a minute, and I walked with Adam out to the sidewalk. "What's up?"

"Bad news," he said. "My parents don't want me 'wasting time' in a band. They're not going to get me a bass after all. Sorry, man. This really sucks."

"Adam, Adam, Adam," I said. "You know what your problem is?"

"What's that?"

"Your problem is that you let The Man run your life . . ."

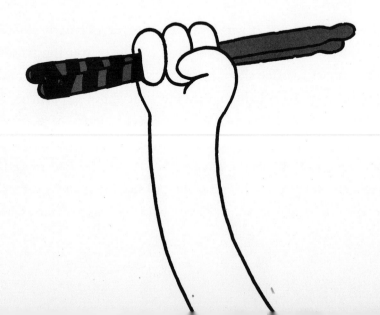